A deadly mistake?

Her capsules . . . could someone have mixed them up with the missing medication? Given her the wrong kind of pills?

Anyone could make a mistake. Even in a hospital. After all, she already knew they'd lost the medication in the first place.

But . . . what if . . . what if it wasn't a mistake? If given to the wrong patient, could those missing pills *kill* someone? Cynthia had said the reason they had to be so careful with the charts was that any mix-up could lead to the wrong medication being dispensed. And she had said that the wrong medication could sometimes result in . . . *death*.

DISCARD

Other Point paperbacks
you will enjoy:

The Invitation
by Diane Hoh

The Accident
by Diane Hoh

Funhouse
by Diane Hoh

The Cheerleader
by Caroline B. Cooney

The Window
by Carol Ellis

Sister Dearest
by D. E. Athkins

YA   Hoh, Diane

HOH   The Fever

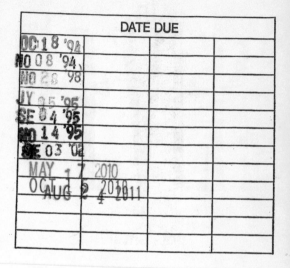

DATE DUE			
OC 18 '94			
NO 08 '94			
NO 26 '98			
JY 05 '95			
SE 04 '95			
NO 14 '95			
SE 03 '02			
MAY 17 2010			
OCT 1 5 2010 AUG 2 4 2011			

ISBN 0-590-45401-3

Copyright © 1992 by Diane Hoh.
All rights reserved. Published by Scholastic Inc.
POINT is a registered trademark of Scholastic Inc.

12 11 10 9 8 7 6 5   3 4 5 6 7/9

Printed in the U.S.A.   01

First Scholastic printing, May 1992

Prologue

Duffy Quinn tosses and turns in a restless, fevered sleep. Hot . . . hot . . . so hot . . . flames burning . . . tormenting her parched, dry skin, setting it on fire . . .

What . . . what is it? Sounds . . . noises . . . ripped into her tortured sleep. No . . . no . . . she doesn't want to wake up . . . no . . . leave me alone, she thinks . . .

Clanging . . . clanging . . . metal on metal . . .

Now a cry, muffled, frightened, "What? What are you — ?"

Now a soft, whispered flapping sound, flap-flap, flap-flap, like gentle waves hitting the shore of a lake . . .

Suddenly another cry, this time filled with terror, "No! Please, don't!"

Hot, hot, burning, blazing . . .

There's a soft thud . . . then silence . . .

Silence floats about the room and then is broken again . . . flap-flapping underneath, rattle-

*clatter-kadunk on top . . . clatter-kadunk, clatter-
kadunk . . .*

Duffy stirs, moans, tries to sit up.

The clatter-kadunk stops abruptly. Silence.

Duffy whispers, "What? What is it?"

*But sitting up is too painful. Duffy sinks back
down against the pillow on her hospital bed, murmuring her question. "What . . . what is it?"*

*The clatter-kadunk begins again. A faint shaft
of light briefly crosses the room as the door creaks
open. The door swings closed again and the light
disappears.*

Silence.

Chapter 1

The hospital stood alone in the center of town. A tall, grim structure of worn gray stone, sparsely covered with wilting ivy, it towered menacingly over the street. The bottom row of stone blocks were mildewed a grimy greenish-black around the base, shielded from the sun's drying heat by a ragged row of hedges. Visitors entering by the wide stone steps puzzled over the thick odor of mold and mildew. They did not realize that the building itself was gradually decaying from the dampness that began at its base and slowly but steadily made its way up the stone.

The upper-floor windows, tall and narrow, stared unblinkingly down upon the street below, as if a sightless gray giant were planting his feet in the uneven grass and boldly inviting strangers to approach . . . if they dared.

Residents of the town of Twelvetrees, Maine, had often remarked sourly that it was not the sort of look a hospital established to welcome the sick and ailing should have.

But they had no money for a newer, more modern building. The old one, unwelcoming as it was, would have to do.

On the fourth floor of Twelvetrees Community Hospital, Duffy Quinn awakened.

The fever had engulfed her, burning her body from the inside out, had transported her to a dizzying world of brilliant reds, hot purples, and blazing yellows. During the long hours since her admission due to a sudden, unexplained fever, the pungent, antiseptic smell of the fourth floor had become her only connection with the real world, as she drifted in and out of a surrealistic carnival of colors.

The smell, which wrinkled her nose even before she was fully awake, dragged her back into an unpleasant reality, a hospital world full of grim whiteness, of chilly, uneasy quiet, of medication, illness, even . . . death.

As depressing as the odor was, it guaranteed that she was still alive, still a part of the real world, no matter how isolated she felt.

As the grogginess of sleep left her, Duffy's head swung instinctively toward the companion bed. It stood silently opposite her own bed, empty and waiting.

Empty . . .

She couldn't have heard anything during the night. There was no one *in* that bed. There hadn't been, not since she was admitted on Thursday night, when her parents had raced to the hospital in the station wagon with Duffy prone on the back-seat, raving weird, nonsensical things, in the throes of a raging, delirium-inducing fever. She remembered nothing about being admitted two nights earlier, but she was certain no one had shared the room even then. The other bed had been empty, and had stayed empty.

What had she heard, then? What had it sounded like . . . the noises? Metal on metal, she remembered . . . like the sound her gold charm bracelet made when it clanked against the metal edge on her desk at school.

Had it been someone out in the hall doing something useful with the old metal bedpans? Newer hospitals had plastic bedpans . . . not so freezing cold. Metal ones *could* make the noise she'd heard.

She was so hot . . . so hot . . . the room was so stuffy, not like at night when they turned off the furnace even though the early spring nights were still chilly. Then the room felt like a refrigerator. Her mouth was so dry, it felt like the cotton balls they swabbed her arm with before they stuck nasty needles into her flesh.

Somewhere within the thick stone walls, water ran. The exhausted plumbing shrieked in agony. The sound of running water made Duffy thirsty. But her hands, the left one impaled by the IV needle steadily feeding her antibiotics, had been robbed of strength by her illness. They floundered around like dead fish on the hills and valleys of her rough, off-white bedding.

What about the other sounds she'd heard? The

slapping sound . . . the rattly, *kadunk*ing sound?

And something else . . . a desperate, terrified cry for help?

No, that couldn't be right. She must have been dreaming.

Hot . . . she was so hot . . . burning . . . burning, as if she were lying on the beach in the middle of July with a cruel sun mercilessly beating down upon her flesh.

She needed water. "Nurse," she murmured, "nurse . . ." Where were all the nurses?

A figure appeared in the doorway. Her doctor. Jonas Morgan. Young, bearded, a gold ring in one ear, sneakers on big feet. Tall, bony, skinny. Not like a doctor at all. Doctors were supposed to be balding or gray. They gave you pills and sent you home. All Dr. Morgan had given her was a battery of tests, thousands of questions . . . and he hadn't sent her home.

He didn't seem to know the first thing about smiling. He frowned a lot, sending thick, shaggy, dark eyebrows on a collision course, and he seemed to take her illness very seriously. She supposed she should be grateful for that, but what she really wanted to do was say, "Lighten up, Doc!"

He took her pulse, listened to her chest, and ordered the nurse who had followed him into the room to take more blood. Duffy groaned. "*Again?* I don't think I have any left. I'm down at least a quart."

He didn't smile. She hadn't expected him to. "We

haven't learned anything yet," he said solemnly, "about what brought you here. It's probably the flu. But we have to make sure."

Minutes later, he was gone, bony shoulders slumped, probably weighted down with the worry of what on earth was wrong with Duffy Quinn.

"Were you in here last night?" she asked the tall, broad-shouldered nurse in white, who took her temperature and then her blood.

"Me? No, hon, I came on this morning at seven. Why?"

"I just wondered. Someone was."

"Another nurse, probably. Your temp has to be monitored."

But no one had taken her temperature. Not when she'd heard the sounds, anyway.

Or *had* they? Maybe she'd just forgotten. Everything was so fuzzy now, with her brain on fire. How could she be sure of anything? Yesterday her mother had told her some of the things she had cried out in her delirium on the way to the hospital. Silly, bizarre things, like warning her mother to get her umbrella out and shouting at her father to change the light bulbs in the kitchen. Crazy stuff.

Maybe last night had just been more of the same.

The nurse took her blood and left, and was immediately replaced by a second nurse, young and pretty, who gave Duffy an expert sponge bath, a clean hospital gown, white with tiny blue flowers, and a delicious back rub.

But she hadn't been on duty the night before,

either, and couldn't tell Duffy anything about who might have been in her room. She, too, said it was probably one of the nurses.

Wouldn't a nurse have answered when Duffy called out?

Amy Severn, a classmate of Duffy's and a Junior Volunteer at the hospital, brought her breakfast tray.

Duffy liked Amy . . . now. At school, Duffy had hardly noticed the quiet, dutiful student, who wore neat, "preppy" clothes like plaid skirts and sweaters, and always had every single blonde hair perfectly in place, sprayed so stiffly each strand looked like plastic. But here, in the hospital where Duffy felt so incredibly helpless, the qualities Duffy would have found uninteresting in Amy in the "outside world" proved comforting. She was kind and helpful, the two things Duffy needed most . . . besides a complete cure, which Amy couldn't provide.

"Are you just getting up, sleepyhead?" Amy asked with a sweet smile as Duffy stirred and moaned. Making a place for the tray on Duffy's cluttered bedside table, she helped the patient struggle to a half-sitting position, which was all Duffy could manage.

"Did you have a bad night?" Amy asked sympathetically as she expertly swung the top of the portable table across the bed and put the breakfast tray on top of it. "Poor Duffy. You've never really been sick before, have you? I can tell. You're not used to lying around with people fussing over you."

Duffy shook her head. It was always so hard

returning to awful reality, waking up and hearing the sounds of the hospital's daytime routine: the rattle of the food carts as they arrived on the fourth floor, the muted thuds of countless rubber-soled shoes, nurses calling back and forth to one another, the squeaking of wheelchairs and, occasionally, someone in pain crying out for relief. And there was, always, the pungent, antiseptic smell of the hospital.

"No," she murmured in response to Amy's comment. "I've never been sick before. Not like this. And I *hate* it!"

Amy's blue uniform whispered crisply as she nodded a head full of stiff curls, neatly held back from her pink, round face by a pale blue ribbon. She took a packet of silverware from the pocket of her uniform and removed the plastic wrapping. Then she slid a bowl of clear soup closer to the edge of the tray. "I know it's awful being sick. Have they taken your temperature yet this morning? Maybe it's gone down." That was Amy . . . forever optimistic.

Duffy made a face of disgust. "I wouldn't know. The nurse who took it wasn't in a sharing mood. I *asked* her what it was. I mean, it is *my* temperature, not hers. But she just shook her head, as if telling me would get her sent to prison or something. It was the nurse with the linebacker shoulders, the one with gray hair."

"Margaret. She's a good nurse, Duffy." Amy's voice was stern.

"Why can't she tell me how I'm doing? Nobody tells me anything around here." Duffy looked up at

Amy. "Amy, couldn't you sneak a peek at my chart? See if my fever's gone down?"

Horror washed across Amy's face. "Duffy! Volunteers are absolutely, positively not allowed to handle the patients' charts. If I got caught even *touching* one, I'd be thrown out of here, and I *love* being a volunteer. Forget it." She unfolded a cheap paper napkin and tucked it under Duffy's chin. "Your doctor will probably tell you about your temp when he comes back in this afternoon."

"No, he won't," Duffy complained. "He never tells me anything, either." But she gave up, knowing she wasn't going to get any information from Amy, who obviously thought that rule-breaking ranked right up there with murder and manslaughter.

Her hands were shaky. The spoon clanked against the bowl. But . . . not the same sound, she told herself. Not the same sound as last night at all. That sound was . . . sharper.

She was so tired. She glared at the bowl of thin, pale liquid staring up at her. "This is my breakfast? It looks like something you'd spray on flowers to kill insects." She gave the bowl a rude shove, sending its contents slopping out across the tray. "If I eat this, I'll barf!"

Amy swiped frantically at the mess with an extra napkin she carried in her pocket.

Of course she carries extra napkins, Duffy thought nastily. But she was grateful that Amy didn't scream at her, or even scold her. All she said was, "Duffy, you have to eat. You have to keep up

10

your strength. You want to get out of here, don't you?"

Duffy's fevered eyes swept around the high-ceilinged, rectangular room. The walls, road-mapped here and there with small cracks, were a dingy white, the windows tall and narrow, shielded by old-fashioned wide-bladed Venetian blinds. The floor had worn black and white tile squares, and she had already memorized every spidery vein in the yellowed ceiling tile overhead. At night, when the hospital was deathly quiet, the grim little room was illuminated only by a tiny nightlight perched beside the heavy wooden door leading to the hall outside and beyond that, the nurses' station.

It was a lonely, isolated place, and Duffy wanted more than she'd ever wanted anything in her life to be free of it.

"Yes," she said softly, "I want to get out of here."

"Well, then, you have to eat. Here, I'll help." Amy sat on the edge of the bed and began to carefully spoon broth between Duffy's fever-cracked lips.

Duffy opened her mouth reluctantly.

Every time the spoon clanked against the bowl, she was reminded of the night sounds she'd heard.

Chapter 2

She had sipped only a few spoonfuls when a husky voice said, "Hey, she's eating! Medical progress is being made in this room today," and a tall boy dressed all in white entered the room, a broad grin on his sharply angled face. "Congrats, Amy! Yesterday, the sight of food made the patient, excuse the expression, puke. You must have magical powers."

Smith Lewis was an orderly at the hospital, but Duffy had seen him around town more than once before she became a patient. His arrival in town several months earlier had sent pulses racing among the female populace at Twelvetrees High School. They didn't get many new arrivals in town. It was the kind of town young people left before the ink was dry on the diploma. So the new arrival, older than they and already out of high school, had been unexpected. And, to most of Duffy's friends, a delightful surprise.

Smith's hair was thick and straight, slightly darker than his eyes, which were the color of root beer. His body moved carelessly, as if he were proud of being tall . . . or proud of being Smith Lewis. Most girls found the proud walk sexy. Duffy found it arrogant.

"Why don't you like him?" Duffy's best friend, Jane Sabatini had asked once when Smith, the top down on his black sports car, passed them in the mall parking lot.

"I didn't say I don't like him. I said I couldn't possibly like him as much as *he* likes him."

She had heard that he was given to practical jokes, which should have endeared him to her, since she had pulled a few pranks herself. But he talked too loudly, drove too fast, and grinned too easily, as if he were saying, "You think I'm adorable, right? Me, too." Every time she saw him, he was with a different girl. It was hard to imagine that someone like Smith Lewis could ever settle down to a medical education and career, which was what someone had told her he planned.

And whether she ate or not wasn't any of his business.

Duffy scowled at him. "I don't need an orderly. Amy's helping me."

Smith shook his head. "Eating hasn't improved your disposition, I see. Too bad. Didn't any of the nurses tell you that being nice to people isn't a bad idea when you look like something washed up on the beach?"

Duffy felt herself flushing and knew it had nothing to do with body temperature. Obnoxious though he was, she knew Smith was right. Her hair felt like an oil slick and she had no makeup on. And although the sponge baths given daily by the nurses were better than nothing, she yearned fiercely for a long, hot shower.

"Leave her alone," Amy told Smith, but she smiled sweetly as she said it. "She's sick. Quit picking on her."

"I just came to get the extra bed," Smith said, ambling over to stand behind the item in question. "You're not using it, and they need it in Pediatrics."

Duffy glanced over at the bed, remembering the night sounds she'd heard. The bed stared back at her. *You were hearing things*, it seemed to accuse. *Can't you see that I'm empty? There was no one here last night but you.*

"Amy," she asked slowly, "that bed's been empty ever since I came in, right?"

Amy nodded. "Sure. You'd remember if you had a roommate, Duffy. The hospital *is* filling up, though. A lot of flu in town. That's probably what you've got." She grimaced, her round, pink cheeks sliding up under her blue eyes. "There's an awful lot to do. And not enough nurses. They've put some of the volunteers on extra hours to help out. I've got band practice, so I can't do it, but Cynthia and a few of the others are helping out." Cynthia Boon was Amy's best friend.

Smith pushed the wheeled bed to the door. "Try to swallow something with sugar in it," he teased Duffy. "A sour female is a sad sight to behold. Take it easy, Duffy Quinn." And he left the room, laughing.

"Pig!" Duffy said heatedly. "A sour female? I should have thrown a pillow at him."

Amy laughed. "Oh, Smith's okay, Duffy. He told me once that his mother named him Smith because it was her last name. She'd always hated having such a boring last name, but thought it would be interesting as a first name. Smith has that same twisted sense of humor. He stole a skeleton from the lab a couple of weeks ago and stashed it in one of the empty beds. That little nurse from the third floor, the one with braids, found it. I guess she almost had a stroke."

Duffy swallowed a laugh. The stunt appealed to her. It was the kind of thing she'd love doing herself. But Smith had said she looked like beach debris. "What a stupid, childish thing to do," she announced primly.

Amy grinned. "Who are you kidding, Duffy? Everyone at school still talks about how you and Kit Rappaport and Jane stole the bust of Walt Whitman from Mrs. Toggle's English room and hung it from the flagpole."

Ignoring that, Duffy asked, "Why didn't Smith get fired? I know the head of the hospital, Dr. Crowder. He doesn't look like he'd have a sense of humor."

Amy shrugged. "Smith did get a lecture. But he told Dr. Crowder it was an experiment. Said he wanted to study the physiological effects of shock." Amy laughed. "Can you believe it? I don't think Dr. Crowder fell for it, but he didn't fire Smith."

Duffy was annoyed with Amy for laughing. She

knew it was only because Amy, usually too stiff-necked to find any humor in rule-breaking, thought Smith was cute. Smith was probably the sort of person who got away with murder, just because of his looks. She hated that. It was so unfair.

"I'd think the nurses would all hate him, he's so obnoxious," she said hopefully.

Amy slid off the bed and picked up Duffy's tray. "Nope. Just the opposite. He's a real hard worker. Sometimes he stays late when he doesn't have to, to help out. He's always hanging around the hospital. The nurses appreciate that, especially right now."

"Amy . . ." Duffy hesitated, not sure how to phrase her question. "Are you absolutely sure there wasn't anybody in that other bed last night? I mean, I was so out of it yesterday. . . . Maybe they brought someone in while I was sleeping, but she got better during the night and went home this morning before I woke up and you came on duty."

Amy frowned. "Duffy, this isn't a hotel. People don't just check in for a few hours. The patient in that bed was discharged last week and it's been empty ever since." Tray in hand, Amy fixed round blue eyes on Duffy. "This is the second time you've asked me about that bed. What's up?"

Duffy shook her head. "Nothing. Only . . . never mind. Forget it." How could she explain what she'd heard when she didn't *know* what she'd heard? She wasn't even sure, in broad daylight, that she'd heard anything. Amy would think brain-rot was setting in.

Maybe it was.

"Look, I've got to go," Amy said. "I'll bring you some magazines later, okay? Is Jane coming this afternoon? Kit?" After Jane, Christopher "Kit" Rappaport was Duffy's closest friend.

"I hope so." What Duffy hated most about being in the hospital, even more than the ugliness, the grimness, and the smell, was the horrible sense of isolation. She missed her friends, her family, her normal routine. This was Saturday. If it weren't for this stupid fever, she'd be home planning a trip to the mall, maybe a movie after dinner. . . . Real life was going on outside these moldy stone walls, and she was no longer a part of it. She *hated* that.

Nodding, Amy turned and hurried out of the room, the skirt of her crisp blue uniform swaying stiffly after her. "Get some rest," she called over her shoulder as she reached the door. "Dr. Morgan says that's the best cure."

Then Duffy was alone in the stuffy silence of her small, dreary prison. She knew Amy was right. Dr. Morgan *had* said, "Rest and quiet, that's the ticket. Sleep restores the body like nothing else can, so get plenty of it and you'll be out of here in no time."

Duffy settled down among the scratchy, yellowed bedding. Of course, Dr. Morgan hadn't added that getting plenty of sleep in a hospital wasn't easy, when nurses and volunteers and orderlies were forever taking your temperature or your blood and giving you baths and emptying your wastebasket or cleaning off your messy bedside table. Sleeping in a hospital was a luxury.

Especially when your room was full of frightening, unexplained sounds that came at night when everyone else had finally left you alone.

She closed her eyes, but she was suddenly afraid to sleep. She didn't want to have the clanking, clattering, flap-flapping dream again. The dream with the cry of terror.

If it *was* a dream. . . .

Chapter 3

Duffy lay in her hospital bed, her pretty, oval face flushed with fever, her eyes on the yellowed ceiling. She couldn't sleep. She flopped over on her side, unmindful of the IV needle embedded in her left hand.

I wish Jane and Kit would hurry up, she thought. If I tell them about my dream last night, Kit will react logically and rationally, the way he always does. Maybe he can help me figure it out.

Kit Rappaport, graduated the year before from Twelvetrees High School, was a math wizard who had been offered several scholarships and turned down all of them to continue working in his uncle's shoe store. The worst fight Duffy and Kit had ever had was about that shoe store.

"You're nuts!" she had shouted, and he had answered, "You just don't get it, do you? I *owe* the man!"

Kit Rappaport had been Duffy's good friend since she was nine. He had come into her fourth-grade class, his reddish hair very like hers except that his was carroty while hers was more cinnamon-colored. His plaid shirt was too small and flapped loosely outside of his jeans, his shoelaces untied. He had taken the seat opposite hers. Halfway through arithmetic, the frog he'd hidden in a pocket escaped and jumped to the floor. Without thinking, Duffy had reached down and scooped it up, hiding it in the folds of her gray sweatshirt before eagle-eyed old Mrs. Lauder could spy it and confiscate it. After class, she had returned the frog to Kit.

They'd been friends ever since, even after Kit skipped ninth grade and moved straight on to tenth, leaving her behind.

They'd never been anything more than friends, although Kit was cute enough, even if he was unaware of it. But he was so wrapped up in the misery of his home life that he had no thought for romance. Orphaned at nine by an automobile accident, he had been taken in by his aunt and uncle. "It's our duty," they told everyone sanctimoniously. Grim, humorless people, without affection or warmth, they believed that children should be useful. So Kit was put to work immediately in his uncle's shoe store, stocking shelves, sorting sizes, and pricing boxes. He hated every second of it.

A day or so after Duffy's argument with Kit about rejecting the scholarships, she had learned the truth from Jane. Upon Kit's graduation, his uncle had demanded that Kit "pay back every cent we've spent on you over the years" by working in the shoe store until the "debt" was paid off.

"Why didn't he tell me?" Duffy shrieked at poor Jane.

"He thought you'd call him a wimp."

Duffy had been ashamed then, because that was accurate. She would have.

Kit told her later he would have ignored his uncle's demands and left town, but his aunt had suffered a heart attack a week after graduation and was unable to help out in the store. He felt then that he had no choice. He would have to stay.

Their friendship had continued. Duffy knew that a lot of her friends didn't understand. Kit was cute and smart and nice. Why wasn't she in love with him? Well, she *did* love Kit, but not the way most girls loved a boy. She loved him because he understood her, her restlessness, her odd sense of humor, even her temper — and he liked her anyway. And she knew he would always be there for her. Even when he finally did go away to college, they'd still be friends. Forever. That was just the way it was.

And if he could get away from the shoe store, he would come with Jane to visit her that afternoon.

She missed him as much as she missed her parents and Jane. He would calm her down, help her to accept the hospital's routine. Kit could do that when no one else could.

"Hi," came suddenly from behind her, and Duffy turned, hope in her gray eyes.

But it wasn't Kit. Or Jane. Instead, Dylan Rourke was standing beside her bed.

A classmate and an employee of the hospital,

Dylan was wearing the obligatory pea-green slacks and tunic. The tunic pulled impatiently at shoulders that spent an hour every day lifting weights and had been used repeatedly as a battering ram on the football field. Dylan's nose had been broken twice in the same spot and now leaned slightly to the right. It gave his square, honest, open face a look of devilishness, which was quickly cancelled out by the trail of freckles leap-frogging across that same nose. Unlike Kit, Dylan had to struggle for good grades, a battle Duffy thought he was losing. That might keep him out of medical school.

Still, while Dylan might not be as smart as Kit, he was shrewd. Working at the hospital part-time put him in touch with doctors who, if he impressed them favorably, could put in a good word for him in pre-med programs at colleges across the country.

One way or another Dylan was determined, like Cynthia and Smith, to become a doctor. Maybe his methods were different, but Duffy had known him since ninth grade and when Dylan wanted something that much, he usually got it. He might look like an ad for a physical fitness magazine, but there was a lot more to Dylan than brawn.

"Your friendly maintenance engineer is here, at your service," he said, grinning, making the freckles dance across the bridge of his nose. His deep blue eyes focused sympathetically on her flushed face. "Anything I can do for you?"

"You mean my friendly *janitor*," Duffy said crankily.

Dylan shrugged good-naturedly. "Whatever.

Duff, you look really sick. You okay?"

Duffy glared at him. "Dylan, would I be in this horrible place if I were okay?" She waved her needle-pinioned hand at him. "This stuff isn't doing a bit of good. I'd get better faster at home, where I belong."

Concern filled his square, open face. "I know you hate it here, Duffy. It's not the greatest place in the world to spend your weekend. But when someone's as sick as you are, this is the safest place to be."

When he turned away to pick up her wastebasket, his broom clanked against the side of the metal container.

That sound last night — was this the same sound?

No. It wasn't quite right . . . it didn't . . . *clank* enough.

"Dylan," she asked, "did you work last night?"

"Uh-uh." He lifted the nearly full basket. "I was wiped out from a chem exam yesterday in Deaton's class. Man, that guy can really dream up some wicked questions! Think I passed, though. No, I wasn't on last night. Why?"

Disappointed that Dylan couldn't help her with last night's puzzle, Duffy sank back against the pillow. "I had this dream . . ." she began. Maybe Dylan *could* help her figure it out. "At least, I think it was a dream. There were these noises . . . it was really bizarre, like there was someone in the room. It was too dark to see, and I was kind of asleep. I was sure someone was doing something in here. But when I called out . . . if I really *did* call out, no one answered me."

Dylan looked interested. "Maybe someone *was* in here. The other bed is gone. Maybe someone was taking it out while you were sleeping and that's what you heard."

Duffy shook her head. "No. Smith just came and got the bed a little while ago. Took it to Pediatrics. And Amy said at breakfast that no one's been in that bed the whole time I've been here, so. . . ."

Dylan thought for a minute. "One of the nurses told me your temperature was headed for the record books when they brought you in. No wonder you've been hearing things. I'm surprised you're not seeing things, too." He stopped and gave her a quizzical look. "You're not, are you? I mean, did you *see* anything last night?"

"No. It was too dark. That little night-light over by the door isn't worth two cents. A jar of fireflies would make a better light."

He laughed. Then he took the wastebasket out into the hall and emptied it into a giant wheeled container.

As he left the room, Duffy sat up straight in bed. There was something . . .

When Dylan returned to put the small basket in its proper place, Duffy commanded, "Do that again."

"What? Do what again?"

"Go out and come back in. Go *on!* Quit looking at me like I just sprouted a second head. I have a good reason. Just do it, please."

Frowning, Dylan obeyed. When he came back in, he said, "What was that all about?"

"It's your *shoes*!" Duffy leaned forward to peer over the edge of her bed. "That's one of the sounds I heard last night . . . that funny slap-slap on the tile. Rubber-soled shoes!"

Dylan was visibly unimpressed. "Duffy," he said kindly, "this is a hospital. Practically everyone wears rubber-soled shoes, so we won't disturb the patients."

Duffy struggled to figure out if she'd just learned anything important. "Yes, but if a member of the staff was in my room last night, why didn't they answer when I called out? There was just this weird, creepy silence."

"You said you weren't quite awake. Are you sure it wasn't a dream?"

Disappointed that Dylan had no better answer than that, Duffy flopped back down on the pillow.

"Hey, don't be mad," he said softly, reaching down to take one of her hands in his. Hers felt parched and dry, his strong and comforting. "Maybe it's your fever. High temperatures can do crazy things to people."

Crazy? *That* wasn't what she wanted to hear.

Seeing the look on her face, Dylan said hastily, "Look, you had to be dreaming, Duffy. If no one was in the other bed, the only reason a nurse would be in this room would be to take care of you. Since you *say* no one was doing that, it's pretty clear that there wasn't anyone here, right?"

"I don't *say* that no one was taking care of me,

Dylan . . . no one *was*. I'm not making this up."

But she didn't want to be mad at Dylan. Especially not over something she herself didn't understand. It wasn't fair to expect Dylan to understand it. They'd been friends a long time. She probably would have dated him once upon a time, but he, like everyone else, had thought she and Kit were a couple, and he'd begun dating Amy Severn. They had broken up only a couple of weeks ago. And he'd been so nice to Duffy since she was admitted to the hospital, she was beginning to wonder if he might be interested in more than friendship now.

She was too sick to think about romance. Besides, how could anybody possibly be interested in someone who looked like roadkill? Dylan was only in her room because he had work to do.

But when she was well again . . . maybe . . .

"I guess you're right," she said after a moment or two of silence. "When my temp spikes, I can't tell the difference between what's real and what isn't. It's like being in another world. A very *hot* one."

Satisfied that she wasn't going to stay mad at him, Dylan began sweeping the room, using his considerable bulk to heave the broom sideways in strong, straight strokes.

"Have you seen Jane or Kit?" Duffy asked.

Dylan glanced at his watch. "Too early for visiting hours. You'll have to wait until after lunch. Isn't he working today?"

Dylan said "he" with a noticeable note of resentment in his voice. He and Kit weren't friends.

Dylan, strong and determined, had been Football. Kit, light and fast, had been Track. Maybe the difference between the two of them was just that simple. Or maybe it went deeper, had something to do with the fact that Dylan was the center of a huge, happy family but had trouble in school, while Kit, who had no family to speak of and lived a lonely, depressing life, had been valedictorian of his graduating class and won scholarships that Dylan would have killed for.

When Dylan talked about Kit, his face suddenly didn't look quite so warm and friendly.

But that only lasted a second. His face cleared quickly as Duffy answered his question.

"I don't know if he's working. I haven't seen him or Jane since I got here. They wouldn't let me have visitors the first day. But it's Saturday. I can't imagine The Grinch Who Stole Kit's Future letting him have a weekend day off. So yeah, he's probably working."

"Kit owed the man," Dylan argued mildly, "he said so himself. He'll go to college next year."

"They brainwashed him. Dumped guilt on him. He should have gone, anyway." But Kit wasn't like that, and both Duffy and Dylan knew it.

When he had finished his task, Dylan came over to the bed to hold her hand in his briefly. Then he said, "Keep your chin up and do what the doctor says, even when you don't want to, okay? I'll be back later to see how you're doing."

The hushed *slap-slap* of his rubber-soled shoes echoed in Duffy's ears for a long time after the sound had faded away. It reminded her . . .

She was being stupid. Of course she'd heard that sound before. As Dylan said, practically everyone in the hospital wore the same kind of shoes.

But if a member of the hospital staff had been in her room last night, why hadn't he or she answered when she called out? Wasn't that what they were there for, to help when help was needed?

What kind of nurse or doctor or orderly or volunteer would ignore a night cry from a patient?

No kind. They wouldn't *do* that. So Dylan had to be right. She'd been dreaming.

But it had certainly *seemed* real.

In an effort to clear her mind of the maddening puzzle, Duffy rolled over on her side and tried to doze until lunchtime and then, she hoped, the arrival of Jane and Kit.

Except for an interruption by the nurse Duffy called "Vampira" because she came in only to collect blood from Duffy's already-sore arm, she remained alone, and finally fell asleep.

Chapter 4

When Junior Volunteer Cynthia Boon entered Duffy's room shortly after the dismal lunch tray had blessedly been taken away, the patient was struggling to force a comb through her tangled, cinnamon-hued waves.

"Oh, I give up!" she cried in despair, heaving the comb across the room. It made a sharp, insulted click when it hit the floor tile. Bouncing twice, it landed in a corner.

"Easy, easy," Cynthia cautioned softly. She walked over swiftly and picked up the comb, returning it to Duffy. "You're not supposed to get upset. Your temperature will spike again."

"Oh, what's the difference?" Duffy grumbled. "I'm never going to get out of this awful place, anyway. I'm imprisoned here for life."

Cynthia, her long, straight, sand-colored hair pulled back in a neat but too-severe bun at the back of her neck, smiled. "Oh, Duffy, you've only been here two days. You should be grateful you don't have a chronic illness, like some of the kids in Pediatrics. They're in and out of the hospital all the time and *they* don't complain."

"Don't lecture me, Cynthia." Duffy hated the way Cynthia looked: her hair so smooth and neat, her pale blue uniform so clean and crisp, her skin shiny and healthy-looking. The only consolation was those tiny lines of tension around Cynthia's pale eyes and full mouth. They made her look older than seventeen years.

Cynthia was the most ambitious person Duffy had ever known and the most energetic. She had probably walked home from the hospital immediately after she was born, unwilling to wait for someone to carry her. Right now, Cynthia was taking her junior and senior years simultaneously because she was so anxious to finish high school and go on to college and medical school . . . which she would probably finish in six weeks or less, Duffy figured.

Duffy glared resentfully at Cynthia. She had almost certainly had a long, beautiful shower and shampoo that very morning. Reason enough to hate her. If she wasn't so nice . . .

"Why can't I have a shower?" Duffy begged. "Cynthia, you could fix it . . . you could sneak me out of here and into the showers down the hall, couldn't you? Please? Smith told me I look like beach garbage, and he's right. He's disgusting, but he's right."

Cynthia shook her neat, narrow head. "Duffy, I know how you feel, but you have to be patient. When Dr. Morgan thinks it's okay for you to have a shower, you'll have one. I'll take you down there myself. But not yet."

"The newer hospitals have showers right in the rooms," Duffy muttered. "But I have to be stuck in this ancient, medieval torture palace where the plumbing screams all day and the elevators creak and — "

"Duffy," Cynthia said gently but firmly as she fluffed Duffy's pillow, "lighten up."

Duffy groaned. "You're right. I'm being a creep. I'm sorry, Cyn. I know I'm a crummy patient. It's just . . ."

"I know. You're not the type to be stuck in a bed, Duffy. It must be making you crazy." Cynthia put on what Duffy called "that hospital face," with the fake smile that failed to reach the eyes, and the voice so falsely cheerful. "But you'll be out of here in no time, I promise." All of the nurses said things like that when a patient was giving them a hard time. It was probably something they learned in the first week of nursing school.

Duffy glowered. "Right."

"Hey, what happened to your other bed? It was here yesterday."

"Smith took it to Pediatrics."

Cynthia marched over to the faded flowered curtain hanging limply on a circular metal rod bolted to the ceiling above the second bed's now-empty space. "Well, then, let's open the window blinds and pull this curtain all the way back. It's blocking the light. No wonder you're depressed." She went first to the window to raise the blinds and then returned to the flowered curtain and yanked it backward on its metal rings.

And Duffy's eyes widened as the curtain sliding along the metal rod made a jingle-jangle sound identical to the one she had heard during the night.

She *had* heard it. She hadn't been dreaming.

She groaned silently. She didn't *want* to be back on this again. Everyone would think she was crazy.

But if someone *had* been in her room. . . .

What were they doing there?

"There *was* someone in here last night," she said aloud.

"Hmm?" Satisfied with the early spring sunshine now flooding the room, Cynthia turned back to Duffy. "What did you say?"

Duffy leaned back against her pillow. "I thought I heard someone in here last night. Dylan told me I'd probably imagined it, because of the fever. I'd just about decided he was right, until you pulled that curtain. Now I *know* I heard something. That curtain was pulled back . . . or forward . . . last night."

Cynthia returned to Duffy's bedside and looked down at her. "I don't get it," she said. "Of course someone was in here. Taking care of you. Your temperature has to be watched carefully. It was *your* curtain you heard, not the other one." She smiled. "We don't have time to waste on empty beds."

Duffy shook her head. "No. Whoever was in here didn't answer when I called out. They didn't want me to *know* they were here. *That's* what's weird, Cynthia."

Before the Junior Volunteer could answer, they were interrupted by the arrival of a short, chunky girl in too-tight Bermuda shorts and an oversized hot-pink sweatshirt, her dark, curly hair carelessly fastened with a huge hot-pink bow. Her face was breathtakingly beautiful, heart-shaped around almost-violet eyes with thick, dark lashes and perfectly arched brows. Her skin was ivory and flawless, as smooth and unblemished as a retouched photograph. She was carrying a pile of magazines and was seriously out of breath.

"Elevator . . . broken . . . again . . ." Duffy's best friend, Jane Sabatini, gasped. "Other . . . one . . . crowded. Had to . . . walk . . . stairs . . ." Her lovely cheeks were flushed with exertion and sweat beaded her upper lip.

"Sit!" Cynthia commanded, shoving a chair at Jane. Jane sat. Cynthia hurried to Duffy's bedside table and poured a glass of water from the heavy metal carafe. "Here, drink this," she ordered, thrusting the glass under Jane's nose. "And next time, wait for a working elevator," she added sharply. "Four flights of stairs carrying a load of magazines is not a smart idea for someone . . ." She stopped, obviously not wanting to be unkind.

"Go ahead, say it," Jane gasped. "For someone overweight. You don't seriously think I'm not aware of it, do you?" An impish grin crossed her lovely face. "You don't approve of exercise, Cynthia? I thought all you medical people preached exercise."

"Nobody recommends that you do it all in one day." Cynthia turned to Duffy. "Look, since you've got company now, I'd better get back to work. I'll report that elevator, Jane. We might actually get lucky enough to have someone fix it. Wouldn't that be a kick?"

Smiling with satisfaction at her own little joke, Cynthia marched from the room.

Jane sighed. "So thin, so efficient, so smart . . . couldn't you just smack her?"

Duffy smiled weakly. "It's even worse when you're stuck in this bed with greasy hair, sweaty skin, and no chance of a shower." Then she added more seriously, "She's been a big help, though. I don't know how she finds the time, but she comes in to see me a lot." She shifted uncomfortably in the bed and then asked, "Where's Kit? Didn't he come with you?"

Jane shook her head and slipped her tired feet out of worn black flats. "Uh-uh. Couldn't get off work. That uncle of his, the one who makes Scrooge look like Santa Claus, has been really riding him lately. Maybe Kit'll be over tonight, if the massah lets the slave out of his chains."

"Poor Kit," Duffy murmured. She was bitterly disappointed. She was glad to see Jane, but she had wanted to talk to Kit about the "dream." She needed his calm, rational input.

Jane nodded. "Anyone else been in to see you?" she asked too casually.

Duffy knew she meant Dylan. Jane had had her

violet eyes on Dylan ever since she'd heard that he and Amy were history.

Duffy knew how lonely Jane was. Her mother had died when Jane was twelve, when Jane's older brother, Dean, had already graduated and gone away to college. Three years later, her father had remarried, but Jane didn't get along with her stepmother.

Popular enough with girls because she was friendly and fun, she had less success with boys, in spite of her beauty. At first, when they'd both started dating, Duffy couldn't understand it. Jane was so gorgeous.

But after watching Jane several times on double dates, Duffy had decided that Jane's problem with boys had to do with her obvious neediness. Jane wanted so desperately to have someone in her life . . . someone who loved her, who thought she was special. The way she latched onto a boy on the very first date, as if they'd known each other forever, as if they were destined to march through life together, was very scary to Duffy.

And obviously very scary to the boys as well.

Duffy had tried talking to Jane about it. "You don't need to go so fast," she had said gently. "You're so gorgeous, Jane, if you'd just relax and take it easy, some neat guy would come along and fall head over heels for you."

But Jane couldn't help it. She was so lonely.

"Yes," Duffy answered, "Dylan was here." And then cringed as disappointment shadowed Jane's face. Because it didn't seem to her that Dylan

Rourke was interested in Jane Sabatini. It seemed to her that Dylan Rourke was interested in Duffy Quinn. That could be a serious problem between two best friends.

But Duffy couldn't think about that now. She had more important things to think about. "Dylan thinks I'm losing it," she told Jane. Then she repeated for Jane her story about the night sounds. "Dylan thinks I was hearing things, because of my fever. Think that's possible?"

Jane shook her head. Several clumps of dark, curly hair escaped the big bow. "It was probably one of those hunks out there in white sneaking in here with a date. I mean, you were probably zonked out, dead to the world, right? All they'd have to do is pull the curtain and they'd have instant privacy. Possible?"

The thought hadn't occurred to Duffy. Since she'd fallen ill, she felt so isolated from the real world. Things like romance and dating and having fun seemed foreign, unreal, as if they existed only on another planet.

But Jane's idea made sense. Two people grabbing a couple of minutes of privacy. She was sure it was against the rules, using a patient's room that way. That would explain why there'd been no answer when she called out. Whoever it was, they wouldn't want to admit they were there.

"I miss you, Duffy," Jane said sadly. "I hate it that you're sick. I know I shouldn't be thinking of myself, but I can't help it. My dad and Susan are busy, my brother's all wrapped up in his wife and kids and his job at the lab, and Kit is being held prisoner by his horrible uncle." Hope edged into her voice. "You do look a *tiny* bit better. Think you might be coming home soon?"

Duffy could do nothing but shrug.

Disappointment again filled Jane's face.

She stayed a long time, most of the afternoon. It was nice to have company, but Duffy, her fever up as it had been the two previous afternoons, tired quickly. When the nurse came in at three-thirty to take her temperature, she sent Jane home. "This girl needs her rest," she said briskly. "Off with you, now!"

It wasn't until Jane, reluctant to leave, had gone that Duffy remembered something that didn't fit Jane's theory about what she'd heard the night before. The whispered protest — had that been the voice of someone nervous about breaking the rules, afraid of being caught?

It hadn't sounded like that. It had sounded much more fearful . . . terrified. There had been so much urgency in that whispered, "No, no, don't!"

What would put such fear into a voice?

Only something very scary. Something terrifying.

Dylan had said she was "safer" here than at home. But the person last night — if there had been someone there — hadn't felt safe.

So maybe Dylan was wrong.

Maybe she wasn't safe here at all.

Chapter 5

The nurse who came in to take Duffy's temperature shortly after another dinner of thin soup frowned as she pulled the thermometer from her patient's mouth and peered down at it. "Doctor isn't going to like this. You're up a whole degree. You haven't been resting like Doctor told you," she accused.

She must think she's in Pediatrics, Duffy thought resentfully, talking to me as if I had a pacifier in my mouth. "I have, too," she replied defiantly, sounding exactly like a two-year-old. That angered her further and she added, "I need to get some exercise, that's all. Anyone would be feverish lying in this stupid bed all day! Why can't I get up?"

"Because you have a fever," the nurse answered patiently. "If you would just do what Doctor says . . ." Then, Duffy's chart under her arm, she turned and left the room.

I've *been* doing what "Doctor" said, Duffy thought, and where has it got me? Nowhere, that's where! What I really need is to get out of this stupid bed, move around, so that my body knows it's still alive. Then it will start acting like it's alive.

Having made up her mind, Duffy decided to wait until after visiting hours for an excursion. The gift shop would be uncrowded then. She'd take the elevator down to the first floor and go buy a magazine and some shampoo. That wouldn't be too much exercise. It would be just enough to get her juices flowing again. Maybe it would even lower her temperature. Then she could go home.

Visiting hours came and went. Apparently sensing that Duffy would rather spend valuable visiting time with her friends, her parents didn't stay long.

But while they were there, she tried once again to talk them into taking her home. "I'm not getting better here," she begged, "and there are all these weird noises when I'm trying to sleep. . . ."

"Sweetheart," her mother said patiently, "Dr. Morgan will tell us when you can go home. It won't be until he's positive that you're well enough. He knows what's best."

And her father added, "You know, Duffy, you scared us half to death . . . our healthy, busy girl lying on the sofa like that, not moving a muscle, your face all flushed with fever. We're not taking any chances by letting you come home too soon."

Gently warning her not to "give the staff a hard time" (they knew her so well), her parents left.

Shortly after they left, Jane arrived, alone. Without Kit. Duffy was filled with disappointment. But before she had a chance to ask Jane where he was,

Cynthia and Amy, now off duty, joined Duffy and Jane. Cynthia looked tired, but Amy seemed as perky as she had earlier in the day.

"I can't stay long," Cynthia confessed, sinking into a wooden chair near the foot of Duffy's bed. "I've got a chem test tomorrow. I'll probably be up all night."

"You work too hard," Amy said gently, settling down beside Duffy on the bed. "Why do you volunteer here when you've got a double load of schoolwork? I *know* why Dylan does it. He needs the contacts here. But you'll slide right into medical school, Cynthia, so why do you spend so much time here?"

Cynthia smiled wearily. "To learn more. Besides, they need the help. They're so understaffed. Especially now, with this awful flu."

Just as Cynthia finished speaking, Smith poked his head in the doorway. "Hey, what's going on? A party? And you didn't invite me?" Without waiting for an answer, he ambled into the room, saying, "Rourke's on his way, too," nodding toward the hall. "He's hot on my heels. All we need now to make this a real party is a couple more guys to even things out."

Ignoring him, Duffy turned to Jane. "Speaking of guys, I thought you'd bring Kit with you."

"I stopped in the shoe store on my way home from here this afternoon, but he wasn't there. His uncle was spitting nails, so I guess they had another fight and Kit didn't show up for work. I don't blame him."

"You talking about Rappaport?" Dylan asked as he arrived, still in his green garb. "He split."

Duffy frowned. "Split?"

"Yeah. Took a hike. Left town. Piled up his car with all his junk and headed for sunny California."

Duffy stared at him. No. No! Dylan was wrong. He had to be. Kit wouldn't take off, just like that. Not without saying good-bye, without explaining. "When? When did he leave?" she cried.

Hearing the distress in her voice, Dylan looked guilty. "Gee, maybe I shouldn't have said anything. I guess I just figured you knew already. I don't know exactly when he left. I ran into him last night. He said he was taking off, leaving. Said he couldn't take his uncle anymore."

"He wouldn't go without telling me good-bye," Duffy said in a soft, bewildered voice. "Not Kit." Then, hope replacing shock, she added, "Maybe he hasn't left yet."

"He's gone, all right," Dylan told her. "His uncle called my dad this morning." Dylan's father was a lawyer. "Said he wanted to cut Kit out of his will. He's not leaving him a penny. He said he didn't see why he should after Kit 'abandoned' him. What an old grouch! Why are you so surprised?" he asked Duffy, his voice kind. "We all knew he couldn't stick it out in that shoe store forever. Who could? Old Man Rappaport's a royal pain. You said so yourself, more than once."

Yes, she had said that. And she'd meant it. She knew the past six months had been rough on Kit. He and his uncle disagreed constantly. And his recuperating aunt was an expert at dishing out guilt. Duffy admired Kit for sticking it out as long as he had, because she knew she never could have done it. In the same circumstances, she would have been throwing dishes, smashing furniture, and screaming her lungs out. And although Kit had seemed to be biding his time with incredible patience, she'd always known that he might bolt at any time.

And now he had.

She didn't blame him. Not the tiniest bit.

But she was sick with disappointment. Not to get a chance to tell him good-bye . . . to wish him luck. . . .

Reading her mind, Cynthia said gently, "Duffy, I'm sure Kit came to tell you good-bye. But you were so out of it, he wouldn't have been allowed to see you. It wasn't his fault. He'll call you when he gets settled, you know he will."

A wave of sadness hit Duffy. Kit . . . gone? She had spent Sunday afternoon with him, in a boat out on the lake. It had been warm when they started out, but then the clouds hid the sun and it became cold and drizzly very quickly. Her mother was convinced it was that outing that had brought on her illness.

Duffy could only hope that if Kit had called the house to see how she was, her mother hadn't accused him of making her sick. He would have felt so guilty.

An uncomfortable silence fell over the room. Realizing it was because she was being so obvious about her feelings, Duffy made an effort to put the bad news aside for the moment. "He'll call me when he's settled in California," she said, blinking back tears. "Cynthia's right. Meanwhile," taking a deep breath, "I've got to get out of this bed. I'm going for a walk the minute the halls are empty tonight. I'm sick of being sick." Then she added in a low voice, "If I hadn't been sick, Kit would have told me good-bye and I could have wished him luck."

As Duffy had expected, both Cynthia and Amy argued with her. She wasn't well enough to leave her room, they said. She'd send her fever soaring, Cynthia pointed out, and Amy said quietly that it wasn't smart to disobey the doctor's orders.

Duffy ignored them. She was getting out of her horrible little room and nothing anyone said would change her mind.

Cynthia and Amy eventually gave up and left. But Jane, anxious to have her friend back at her side, said, "I think it's a great idea. Just don't overdo it."

Although she could tell that Dylan and Smith both disapproved of her plan, they knew better than to argue with her, and shaking their heads, they left with Jane.

When Duffy first sat up and swung her legs over the edge of her bed, the room turned bright pink and swayed around her. That passed. When her vision had cleared, she slipped her feet into white terrycloth slippers and wrapped herself in a matching robe. Then she stood up.

Red waves of heat slapped at her, blurring her vision again. One step . . . if she could just take one step without falling . . . tentatively, she put a foot forward, gripping her IV pole for support.

She was still standing. Another step, then another, and soon she was at the door.

Peering out, she found with satisfaction that the hallway was deserted. Silent and empty. No nurses, no visitors, no orderlies, no patients. She had the hall all to herself.

It was great being out of bed, although she felt like a toddler taking its first steps. Her legs threatened to cave in at any moment. But she was too eager to be free of her prison, and moved slowly and carefully out into the long, narrow hall.

"You don't like being cooped up, do you?" Smith Lewis asked her softly as he appeared out of nowhere.

She jumped, startled, and slammed into the wall. Her plastic IV bag slapped against the metal pole. "Don't *do* that!" she hissed, furious.

"I don't blame you," he said, ignoring her anger. "Being cooped up would make me crazy, too."

Crazy? Sensitive to the word because of her confusion about last night's strange sounds, she snapped, "I'm not crazy! Being cooped up isn't making me crazy, and neither is my fever."

Smith raised his hands in front of him in mock defense. "Whoa! Easy, girl. Chill out." And shaking his head, he moved forward to take her elbow. "I just wanted to make sure you could handle this little hike. You look pretty shaky to me. Your legs going to hold up?"

Duffy was ashamed of herself for biting his head

off. Being so unsure about what had really happened the night before *was* making her crazy. But she didn't want Smith to know that.

"I've changed my mind," she said suddenly. "The nurse was right. I'm not up to this. Would you help me back to my room, please?" If she was going to take her little "hike," she was going to take it alone. She didn't want Smith Lewis hanging on her, as if she were some feeble old lady. She'd get rid of him first, then she'd get her exercise.

But before she left her room a second time, she'd make absolutely sure no one was around. Especially Smith.

"This Kit person," he said as he accompanied her back to her room, "someone special to you?"

She didn't think she could talk about Kit without crying, and she had no intention of crying in front of Smith Lewis. "A friend," she said, her voice strained.

"Just a friend?"

"Just" a friend? No, much more than a friend . . . but she didn't want to talk about Kit with Smith. "A good friend," was all she would say.

"Oh. Great."

He left her at the door to her room and disappeared down the hallway.

After checking her pocket to make sure she had money for a magazine and shampoo, Duffy peered into the hall again. A nurse came out of the shower room with a patient. Duffy ducked back behind her door. A shower — how wonderful! Maybe, if the exercise regulated her temperature the way she hoped it would, she could talk someone into letting her take a shower the next day so she could wash her oil-slicked hair and look like a human being.

When the hall was finally deserted again, the overhead fluorescent lights dimmed for the night. The nurses' station was empty. Murmuring voices from other rooms told her the staff was busy readying patients for the night. Now was the time to make her dash for freedom.

She scuttled down the hall quickly and quietly, sliding the IV pole along behind her like a puppy on a leash.

One of the elevators wore an OUT OF ORDER sign. Duffy remembered Jane's heavy breathing that afternoon. Poor Jane.

Duffy pushed the button for the working elevator and waited impatiently for the silver arrow over the door to point to the number four. As the arrow began to move upward, Duffy stepped closer to the wide metal doors, prepared to enter as soon as they slid open.

The arrow moved, turtle-slow, around its half circle.

Gripping her IV stand, Duffy took another step forward.

The elevator finally reached her floor, and the doors, groaning with the effort, began to slide open.

"Duffy!" a voice off to her right shouted. "*Stop!*"

As her right foot lifted to step onto the elevator floor, Duffy turned her head to see who had shouted at her. She had no intention of letting anyone stop her little journey, and continued to aim her foot into the elevator.

But before it could land, a blur of white flew through the air and collided with her, knocking her off-balance and sending her flying backward. Too startled to cry out, she landed on her back on the tile floor, half-smothered by the white projectile now sprawled across her. Trying to catch her breath, Duffy realized in stunned shock that the bulk pinning her down had hair . . . arms . . . legs . . .

Smith Lewis.

Smith Lewis had just tackled her bodily in the hospital hallway and sent her flying across the tile.

"You're insane!" she gasped, struggling to sit upright. "You maniac! What are you *doing*?"

He pushed himself up into a sitting position. "Look!" he breathed, pointing a shaky finger toward the elevator. "Look!"

Duffy's eyes followed the pointing finger.

The elevator's doors were open all the way.

But there was no elevator cage inside.

There was only a black, yawning void.

Chapter 6

Duffy slumped against the wall, her shoulders shaking as Smith stood up and bent to retrieve her overturned IV pole.

"There . . . isn't anything *there*," she said dully, her eyes on the wide black mouth waiting to swallow her up. "I . . . I would have stepped into . . . air. Nothing but *air*!"

"And fallen five floors to the basement," Smith agreed grimly. His voice was full of anger and contempt as he added, "This is Rourke's fault. I *told* him it was the *second* elevator that wasn't working, *not* the first. He put the sign on the wrong one!" Shaking the thick thatch of dark, curly hair, he said, "Someone could have been killed." He moved his gaze from the black gaping hole to Duffy. "*You* could have been killed," he said emphatically.

As he moved to set her IV pole upright and then help her to her feet, he muttered, "Wait'll I get my hands on that Dylan! I'll have his head on a platter. His supervisor's going to hear about this, too."

Duffy couldn't tear her eyes away from the empty

elevator shaft. Empty. No cage there to carry her safely down to the first floor. Nothing there but a deep, hungry emptiness. For one horrible second, she could actually feel herself falling . . . falling . . . into the shadowy nothingness. A sickening, terrifying sense of helpless horror overwhelmed her.

Duffy stood up. If it hadn't been for Smith's firm grip on her elbow, her knees would have buckled and sent her to the floor in a slow, buttery slide.

A nasty little voice in her mind chimed repeatedly, *You almost died . . . you almost died . . . you almost died. . . .*

"What on earth is going on here?" a voice demanded. The night nurse bustled down the hall toward them, indignation written all over her middle-aged face. "What are you two doing out here? Lewis, you're not on the schedule tonight. And Quinn, what are you doing out of bed?"

Shock and fear had stolen Duffy's voice from her. She was unable to speak.

Smith quickly explained what had happened as briefly as possible. "I came back to get my paycheck," he added. "It wasn't ready when I left earlier. And I saw Duffy about to step into the elevator, the one I knew was out of commission."

"Oh, for heaven's sake," the nurse said in an exasperated voice, "that elevator was supposed to be fixed by now." She took Duffy's arm. "You take care of that sign," she ordered Smith briskly. "I'll see that Quinn gets back to her room."

Duffy found her voice. "Smith," she said quietly as he moved away, "thanks. Thanks for — "

"Forget it," he interrupted. "No big deal. Go back to bed. And," he added harshly, "maybe you'd be better off staying there. Safer that way."

Nodding, Duffy allowed herself to be led back to her room.

"You've got no business being out of bed," the nurse scolded as Duffy crawled into bed. "You look flushed. I'm going to take your temperature right now. Then you'll have your sleeping pill so you can forget all about this nasty business."

Duffy didn't see how that was possible. How could she forget that she had almost plunged five floors to her death?

I came to this horrible place to get well, she thought as the thermometer was thrust under her tongue, and instead, I almost died.

How could Dylan have made such a terrible mistake?

She lay curled up in bed, trembling violently, until the sleeping pill began to take effect. Her body relaxed, involuntarily. Her arms and legs turned to warm water. But her mind continued to shudder with fear, until that, too, fell under the spell of the drug.

She was drifting off into a pleasant cotton-candy fuzziness when Smith came quietly into the darkened room and stood beside her bed.

Leaning down, he asked softly, "You okay?"

"If you get caught in here," she said drowsily, "Attila the Nurse will have you shot. She just left, but she could pop back in at any time, probably with a whip in her hand or a set of thumbscrews."

Smith didn't smile. "They gave you a shot? Or a pill? Must have. I expected to find you in hysterics. Medication is a wonderful thing." He awkwardly patted her head, said, "Sleep well," and turned to leave.

But there was something Duffy needed to ask him, if she could only grab the thought dancing around crazily in her mind and turn it into coherent words. The question she needed to ask Smith was . . . was . . .

No, the sleeping pill was getting in her way, making it impossible to form the question into words and send it on its way to Smith.

It would have to wait until tomorrow. She hoped it wasn't important.

But she had a strong, uneasy feeling that it was.

In spite of the uneasiness, she was asleep before Smith reached the door.

When she awoke Sunday morning, having slept soundly through the night, the question had crystallized in her mind. It was so clear and so urgent, she asked the nurse who brought her breakfast tray if Smith was on duty.

The nurse, a young, pretty student, grinned. "You, too? All the other female patients are ga-ga over Lewis. I don't see him as your type, but — "

"It's not like that," Duffy protested, annoyed. "I just need to ask him something."

"Right. Like what he's doing next Saturday night, just in case you're sprung by then?"

Duffy glared daggers at the girl. "Will you just

call him for me, please? Tell him I need to see him, right away."

Although the student nurse was grinning when she left the room, she must have passed on the message, because five minutes later, Smith hurried into the room.

"Well, you look better. Your eyes are still sort of glazed with terror, though. What's up?"

"Smith," Duffy said earnestly, "when exactly did you tell Dylan to put the out-of-order sign on the elevator?"

Smith thought for a minute. "About four o'clock. Right after that friend of yours, Jane, had to struggle up four flights of stairs. I was afraid someone would have a heart attack before maintenance got the cage fixed. Why?"

"Well, think about it," Duffy said impatiently. "This place was full of visitors all afternoon and all evening. People were going up and down like yo-yos. If Dylan's sign was hanging on the wrong elevator all that time, how come no one but me came so close to taking a dive into an empty elevator shaft?" She shuddered just thinking about it.

Smith moved closer and sat on the edge of her bed. "You're right," he said slowly. "It doesn't make any sense."

"Unless . . ." Duffy began, "unless Dylan *did* put the sign on the right elevator and somebody moved it just before I got there."

Smith looked skeptical. "Why would someone move it?"

"How should I know? But they must have."

He thought for a minute and then said, "I just thought of something. Day before yesterday, the *other* elevator was screwed up. It was fixed right away. I guess it's possible that someone who came in late today wouldn't have expected the repairs to be made so fast. And they wouldn't have known the second one had broken down. So, when they came in today and saw that sign, they would have thought it was a mistake. And they would have moved the sign . . . back to the elevator they *thought* was still broken."

"Someone who had the day off wouldn't have known the broken-down elevator had been repaired?" Duffy echoed. "Don't you people *tell* each other things?"

"I'm talking about when the guy came in, first thing, before he'd talked to anyone. Some of the crew comes on at nine P.M. I know Elmer Dougherty came in at eight last night, just before you left your room. He could have switched the sign, thinking someone had put it on the wrong cage."

"I guess that makes sense. Can you find out for sure?"

Smith nodded. "I can find out who, besides Elmer, had Thursday off. I'll ask around, see who else came in late yesterday, find out if they switched the sign." He grimaced. "I'm glad I didn't read the riot act to Rourke. I don't think I want him mad at me. He works out regularly. My idea of exercise is draping myself over the wheel of a sportscar." He stood up. "Take it easy today, okay? You still look a little shaky to me."

Glad that the mystery had been solved, Duffy watched him go. He *was* thinner than Dylan. But he was taller, and she liked the way he moved, so easy and careless, as if he wasn't afraid of anything.

But then, he hadn't almost fallen into a deep, black hole last night, she thought with some resentment. He could afford to walk as if he didn't have a care in the world.

Kit had walked the same way. He wasn't afraid of anything.

She, on the other hand, would probably start shaking violently from now on every time she went near an elevator.

Shuddering, Duffy closed her eyes.

Chapter 7

Dr. Morgan had already heard about Duffy's brush with death by elevator but seemed concerned only with how the near-accident had affected her illness. "I didn't give you permission to get out of bed," he reprimanded her sternly. "If you're not going to follow my orders, how do you expect me to help you?"

By fixing the elevators when they break, Duffy wanted to say, but she didn't. She was feeling totally crummy, hot, and sick. The IV needle pinched her hand unmercifully.

Noticing the stiff way she held the limb, Dr. Morgan said in a softer voice. "Maybe we can get rid of that for you soon. Would that help?"

It would definitely help.

But the IV was still in when the doctor and the nurse who had accompanied him into the room and taken Duffy's temperature left.

Amy and Cynthia were horrified when they heard what had happened to Duffy, and came rushing to her room the minute they had a break in their duties. Jane, taking advantage of Sunday morning's visiting hours, arrived at almost the same time. She paled visibly when she heard what had happened.

"Oh, Duffy," she said, her flawless skin as white as Duffy's sheet, "you could have . . . you could have been . . . killed." Her violet eyes filled with tears at the thought of losing her best friend. "What if someone hadn't been there to save you? What if Smith hadn't been around?" Weakened by the thought, she sank into the wooden, straight-backed bedside chair.

"She's right, Duffy," Amy agreed. "You owe Smith. If it hadn't been for him . . ."

Duffy didn't like the idea of "owing" Smith Lewis, but she knew Amy was right. She shuddered. "I keep seeing that black hole . . ." Taking a deep breath, she changed the subject. "I am," she announced in a relatively steady voice, "going to take a shower this afternoon if it's the last thing I do. It's the only thing that will make me feel better. I deserve it, after what happened, right?"

"Didn't you learn anything last night about disobeying doctor's orders?" Cynthia asked brusquely. "Honestly, Duffy, you are the worst patient in the world!"

And Amy added hesitantly, "Duffy, you can't take a shower with that IV in your arm."

"They're going to take it out. Dr. Morgan said so."

Cynthia shrugged. "Well, do as you please, Duffy. You will, anyway. But don't blame me if someone catches you in the act and yells at you."

"You'd better not rat on me," Duffy warned. "Any of you. If you do, and I miss my shower, I'll jump off the top of this stupid building. And then I'll haunt you guys for the rest of your natural lives."

Jane laughed. "Oh, Duffy, you're the least likely person in the world to jump off a building . . . unless it's because you've rigged up some fancy parachute and you want to try it out."

When the three had gone, promising to return that afternoon, Dylan arrived, bearing a healthy green plant in a white ceramic swan, purchased in the downstairs gift shop.

After thanking him for it, she asked him about the out-of-order sign. "Did you put it on the elevator at four o'clock, when Smith told you to?" she asked.

"Of course I did!" Dylan's words oozed injured pride. "Why? Did Lewis say I was goofing off?"

"No, and don't be so touchy. Did you put the sign on the first elevator or the second?"

"The second. That's the one Lewis said wasn't working. Why are you asking so many questions? What's going on?"

"No one told you I almost fell into the empty shaft of the broken elevator last night?" Duffy knew the story had circulated through the hospital rumor mill. That was how Cynthia and Amy had heard it.

"I just got here," Dylan answered. "I haven't talked to anyone. I went to the gift shop and then came straight here."

She told him about her narrow escape. And then,

while he sat, shocked and silent on her bed, she added Smith's theory about how the sign had been innocently switched.

"Elmer Dougherty was off on Thursday," Dylan mused. "I think Pete Ramsey was, too. And Smith could be right. Neither of them would have expected the first elevator to be fixed so fast, especially when they weren't here to do it. They don't think much of the other two maintenance guys. They're always complaining about them. So yeah, Elmer or Pete could have moved my sign." Dylan looked at Duffy, concern in his blue eyes. "You sure you're okay?"

"I'm fine." That wasn't true. She wasn't fine. Every time she thought about how close she had come to diving into that deep black hole her heart pounded and she felt dizzy and breathless. She didn't think that feeling would ever go away completely.

"Thanks for the plant," she told Dylan. "You'd better get to work. I don't want to get blamed if you're late."

He surprised her by kissing her before he left, bending to touch her cheek lightly with his lips. "You do feel a little bit cooler," he said as he straightened up. "Maybe they'll let you go home soon."

"The sooner the better. I've already made up my mind that I'm *taking* a shower whether anyone says I can or not. Tonight. Even if I have to sneak down the halls like a criminal."

"Good idea. It'll help you keep cool. Take it easy."

When Dylan had gone, Duffy lay with her eyes wide open, wondering why Smith hadn't come back to tell her who had moved the sign.

When the nurse came in to take her temperature, she beamed down at Duffy and said, "I've got good news."

"My temperature's normal and I can get dressed and go home," Duffy offered, a false note of hope in her voice. She didn't feel *that* cool.

"No, afraid not. But I have orders to remove your IV. That should cheer you up. Your doctor wants to try you on antibiotic capsules in place of the intravenous. So I can take this nasty thing out of your arm. That should be a relief."

It was. Free of the painful pinching sensation, Duffy gently rubbed the football-shaped black-and-blue mark left by the needle.

"Here," the nurse said, shaking a tiny fluted paper cup, "these should do the trick. Take two now, and I'll give you more when it's time."

"So when do I get sprung?" Duffy asked when she'd obediently swallowed the capsules.

"That's up to your doctor. I think he's waiting to see if you develop additional flu symptoms, just to be sure that's what you've got. So far, your blood tests have been negative." She glanced out the window. "The doctor even said you could go outside if you wanted, get some fresh air. Get one of the orderlies to take you. In a wheelchair, of course. And *don't* get out of the chair. Not yet. It's too soon."

When the nurse had gone, Duffy aimed her own gaze out the tall, skinny window. It was a sunny, blue-skied early spring day. She was sick to death of her grim prison. If she could get someone to wheel her outside . . .

Her legs were newborn-weak when she slid from her bed. But since she would be in a wheelchair, it didn't matter that her legs, like everything else in this hospital, weren't functioning properly.

The only orderly out in the hall was Smith. He was advancing toward her, pushing a wheelchair.

"You're supposed to take me outside," Duffy commanded as he reached her doorway. She was annoyed with him for not getting back to her with the information she wanted. She still didn't know for certain that he was right about how the sign on the elevator had been switched.

Smith laughed. "No kidding? And here I was planning on pushing this empty chair up and down the halls all day, because it's so much fun. Now you've gone and spoiled my plans."

"Why didn't you come and tell me who switched that sign?" Duffy hissed, climbing into the chair. "I've been waiting for hours!"

"Because I didn't find out anything," he answered amiably, coming around behind her to begin pushing her down the hall. "No one could remember moving the sign. Or maybe they were afraid to say, considering what almost happened. Probably thought they'd be in hot water if they admitted moving it. Sorry."

Duffy sulked in disappointment. She had hoped to prove that Dylan hadn't made a mistake. She didn't like thinking that he'd put the sign on the wrong elevator. "Maybe you didn't ask the right questions," she accused.

But before he could answer, she realized that they were headed toward the elevator.

Her body began trembling violently, rocking the wheelchair.

"Whoa!" Smith said, leaning down to look into her face. "You okay?"

"No," Duffy whispered. "No. I can't go in there. I can't ride in that elevator. Take me back to my room."

"Look," he said patiently, "you want to go outside, right? You have to go downstairs to do that, right? The only way I can get you downstairs is on the elevator. C'mon, relax! I'll park your chair back against the wall and make absolutely sure the cage is there before I push you over to the door, okay?"

Duffy couldn't control her shaking or the trembling of her lower lip or the nausea that rose in her stomach. The thought of those big metal double doors opening again terrified her.

But she wanted so much to go outside, to get out of this building, out of her room.

"Don't move it one inch away from the wall until you're sure that cage is there," she ordered from between teeth chattering with anxiety. "Promise?"

"I promise. Try to relax, okay? You shouldn't be getting upset like this. Could send your temperature up again and you'll never get out of here."

When he parked her chair against the wall, several feet from the elevator doors, she closed her eyes. When she opened them the cage was there, just as it should be. Smith wheeled her in, and kept one hand on her shoulder the whole way down. That helped.

"I can't stay out here with you," Smith said as he wheeled her around a corner of the building. "I've got things to do. But I'll be back in half an hour or so. I'm supposed to remind you *not* to move from that chair. Doctor's orders. So, no jogging, okay?"

Her bad mood broken by the bright sunshine and blue, cloudless sky and the faint April breeze, Duffy nodded. "I won't move, I promise. Park me anywhere here." Then, feeling guilty for her earlier rudeness, she added gratefully, "And thanks. The fresh air feels great."

"It'll probably do more good than those capsules you're taking," Smith agreed. Then he set the brake on her wheelchair and, whistling, left her alone.

Duffy relaxed in the old wooden wheelchair. She was seated at the top of the steep slope carpeted in bright-green new grass. Other patients sat in similar chairs, reading or talking to one another. Far below her, where the slope ended, she could see silvery-blue water glistening in the sunshine. The lake — the only pretty part of the hospital grounds. Several children were sailing boats in the water and a pair of workmen in jeans and white T-shirts were planting new shrubbery around the lake's shoreline.

It felt wonderful to be part of the real world again. I almost feel human, Duffy thought, a half smile on her face. My IV is gone, and I'm actually outside, away from that horrible room and those grungy halls. I wish I could wheel this chair all the way home and never come back here again.

She couldn't do that. But she could relax and enjoy the time she had outside.

She slid down in the chair, trying to find a comfortable sitting position so that she could tilt her face up toward the sun in hopes of getting an early start on her tan.

A noise that startled her came from somewhere behind her. Just as she turned her head to locate its source, the wheelchair jerked abruptly, lurched forward, and began slowly moving down the slope.

Duffy bolted upright in the chair. It wasn't supposed to be moving. It was supposed to be *parked*. Sitting safely in a stationary position. Safe. Safe and unmoving.

Instead, the wheels continued to revolve. As they turned, they picked up speed.

"Hey!" a student nurse studying in the sun cried out in surprise as she glanced up and saw the wheelchair bearing down upon her. "Hey, stop that thing!"

Duffy, her mouth open in shock, had no idea how to stop it.

The student nurse managed to throw herself out of the way just in time. A second later, the heavy chair careened across the blanket she'd been sitting on. "Hey!" she shouted after it, "what's the big idea?"

Other shouts joined hers as the wheelchair, with Duffy in it, rolled faster and faster down the hill. When it reached the steepest part of the slope and tilted precariously forward, Duffy had to cling to the wooden arms with every ounce of her strength to keep from being thrown out across the hill. Slamming out onto the ground now would break every single bone in her body.

With a sinking heart, Duffy realized her mistake. She should have jumped from the chair the second it began to move. At the top of the slope where the ground was level, she would have sustained only a few minor bumps and bruises. But she had been so startled by the sudden, unexpected movement, that she hadn't been thinking clearly.

Now, it was too late. Her hands fumbled frantically near the wheels, searching for the brake, but she couldn't find it. And the fear of crushing her fingers in the speeding wheels brought her hands back up to clutch the chair arms again.

She tried to scream. But the wind ripped viciously at her mouth, stealing her voice.

"Help me, help me, help me," she mouthed desperately as the chair tore down the slope. Her terrified heart pounded in her chest, her knuckles turned white on the wooden arms, her lips moved soundlessly, frantically, as she tried in vain to scream for help.

The lake, glistening in the sun, beckoned below. Duffy was headed straight for it. The water, this early in spring, would be freezing cold. If the chair dove into the lake, it would sink like a stone, and she with it. Even if someone saved her from drowning, exposure to that freezing water would set her illness back weeks. It might even kill her.

Suppose she got tangled in the wheels, under-water?

Here and there across the hillside, people raced to her rescue, waving their arms and shouting.

None was close enough to reach her in time.

Why couldn't she scream? Why was the wind stealing her voice? "Help, help, help," she mouthed over and over again as the chair sped down the slope, closer and closer to the icy waters of the lake.

The two workmen glanced up in astonishment and, without dropping their shovels, dove out of the way of the heavy wooden chair barreling down upon them like a missile.

In utter despair, Duffy moaned helplessly and closed her eyes.

Chapter 8

As the runaway chair, holding Duffy prisoner, continued its suicidal dive toward the chilly waters of the lake, she gave up hope. She was going into that lake . . . no way to stop it . . . no way . . . so cold . . . it would be so cold. . . .

Eyes closed against the terrible reality of it, lips mouthing frantic prayers, she shrank into a little ball curled up against the back of the chair and clenched her teeth. She would have to swim for it.

Duffy opened her eyes and was instantly blinded by the glare of the water just inches away from the speeding chair. She sprang upright, leaning forward, preparing to dive the instant the chair left land.

And she nearly catapulted out over the water as the wheelchair jolted to an abrupt, grinding halt at the very edge of the lake. Her head snapped to one side. She gasped as the chair jerked backward, tilted slightly, its wheels spinning frantically, and then settled shakily onto the sand.

When the chair finally sat sullenly and completely

still, Duffy sagged against its back. Her chest heaved in an effort to restore normal breathing.

"You okay?" Dylan's voice whispered in her ear. "You okay, Duff? All in one piece?" And then he was there, kneeling beside her, taking her shaking hands in his, gazing up into her face with worried eyes.

She couldn't speak. Her breath came in ragged gasps. Her eyes remained fastened in bewildered horror on the cold, silvery water. Then tears of hysteria began pouring down her cheeks, spilling over her lips and chin. "Oh," she whispered numbly, "oh, oh . . ."

"Man, that chair weighs a ton!" Dylan exclaimed as staff members and patients alike began to gather around Duffy, expressing concern for her safety. "No wonder you couldn't stop it on your own. For a minute there, I didn't think I was going to be able to, either."

Dylan had saved her life. He'd risked being pulled into the water right along with her and the runaway chair. He had saved her. If only she could stop shaking and crying long enough to thank him.

"Thanks," she whispered, her tear-streaked face crumpling as the realization that she was safe began to sink in. "Thanks, Dylan." Then she hid her face in her hands, her body trembling from head to toe.

The group of onlookers, uneasy with their inability to comfort her, murmured among themselves. One said in a low voice, "She needs a doctor," and turned to run up the hill.

Smith Lewis, followed closely by Amy Severn,

came running down the hill. "What's going on?" Smith asked angrily as they arrived at the foot of the hill. "I thought I told you to stay where I put you," he began to accuse Duffy, and then realized the state she was in. "What happened?" he asked Dylan. "What's wrong with her? How did she get down here?"

"Take it easy, Lewis," Dylan warned, putting his hands protectively on the back of the wheelchair. "Duffy's had a really bad time. Did you check the brake on this chair before you left her?"

Smith flushed angrily. "Of course I did, Rourke. I checked it twice." His voice rose. "What *happened*?"

Then everyone began talking at once, a jumble of excited voices. None of it made any sense. Smith looked more confused than ever.

Duffy, her eyes glazed with shock, said numbly, "The chair ran away. It just . . . took off. If it hadn't been for Dylan, I'd . . ." Fresh tears began to flow. "If it hadn't been for Dylan, I'd be in the lake right now." Her voice broke, "Oh, God, I came so close . . ."

Smith looked stupefied. "Ran away?"

"Yeah," Dylan said. "Took off. Escaped. Straight down the hill. With Duffy still in it."

"Dylan saved my life," Duffy said softly. "Can I go back to my room now, please?"

Smith's flush changed to pallor as he lifted his head to survey the steep distance the chair had covered so quickly. "You . . . you came down *that* hill in a wheelchair?"

"Yes, she did," Dylan answered emphatically, "and I think she should have her doctor check her out. Everyone move out of the way, please, so I can take her back inside."

"Yes," Duffy said, trying in vain to tear her gaze away from the sun-glistening lake. "Yes. I want to go back inside."

"Duffy," Smith said quietly, looking down at her with guilt-filled eyes, "I was sure I checked that brake. I'm sorry."

A fellow orderly standing by offered loyally, "Wasn't your fault, Lewis. Those brakes aren't much good. The chairs are ancient. Old Man Latham donated them years ago when he first came on the hospital board."

But Smith looked unconsoled.

Duffy wanted to tell him to forget it. But how could she, when she knew *she* never would. Never . . . never. That race down the hill . . . feeling so helpless, so terrified . . . she knew she would feel the harsh wind slapping against her face in nightmares for a long time to come.

I'm not dead, she thought with a sense of morbid wonder. I'm not dead . . . but I almost was. Again. For the second time in two days, I almost died.

How was that possible in a place where she had come to get well?

Duffy's doctor found no sign of physical damage, but the look on the nurse's face when she removed the thermometer from Duffy's mouth signified bad news.

"Your temperature's shot back up," she said briskly, shaking the glass tube back down to normal before replacing it in its antiseptic holder. "Small wonder, after what you've been through. The whole hospital's abuzz. Here," extending one of the tiny paper cups with pills in it, "take these and try to get some rest. I'll look in on you in a little bit."

Amy and Cynthia stayed with Duffy until her parents and Jane arrived.

Amy's eyes were wide with shock. "Oh, Duffy," she whispered in awe when the nurse had gone, "you must have been terrified! I can't believe how lucky you were!"

Cynthia, sitting at the foot of the bed, nodded in agreement.

Duffy settled more deeply beneath the covers, hoping to still her trembling limbs. She stared at Amy. "Lucky?" she whispered. "Lucky?" She closed her eyes, trying to blot out the sight of that lake rushing closer and closer to her.

Amy turned a deep pink. "Well, I know it was terrible, what happened to you," she stammered. "What I meant was, you didn't go into the lake. Dylan stopped you, just like Smith stopped you from stepping into the empty elevator shaft. That's what I meant by lucky."

"Amy," Duffy said, her voice quivering, "this place isn't safe for me. I have to go home, right now, before something else terrible happens to me. Ask my doctor, okay? Tell him . . . tell him it's absolutely crucial that I not spend another night in this horrible place." Tears of fear and despair filled her eyes. "Please, Amy?"

Matching drops of saltwater trembled on Amy's own pale lashes. She couldn't speak.

"Duffy," Cynthia said, folding and refolding an edge of Duffy's yellowed blanket. "I know you've been through some really awful stuff. But it isn't the *hospital's* fault. The hospital isn't out to get you. You've just had a couple of accidents, that's all. You were in the wrong place at the wrong time. It could have happened to anyone."

"But it *didn't*." A sudden wave of nausea washed over Duffy, and her head began to ache. "It happened to *me*. And . . . and I just remembered . . . there was this weird noise . . . right behind me . . . just before the chair took off down the hill. I'd forgotten . . . but I remember now. This sound . . ."

Amy leaned forward. "Noise? What kind of noise?"

Duffy needed to sleep. She could barely keep her eyes open. She struggled to remember what kind of noise it had been. "I'm not sure . . . like someone was tiptoeing up behind me . . . you know, the way people walk when they don't want to be heard? And then . . . a little creaking noise . . . the sound those old chairs make when the brake is put on . . . or . . . *off*." Duffy's eyes flew open. "Amy! That *is* the sound I heard . . . the brake being released on my chair!"

Amy and Cynthia exchanged glances.

"Duffy," Cynthia said patiently, "that's silly. I know you're upset, but you're really beginning to sound paranoid. Anyone fooling around with your chair would have been seen by the other people outside."

Duffy fought rising nausea. "Maybe not. I was at the top of the hill. Alone. Everyone else was on the slope. Why would they be watching me? Someone could have run up behind me, released the brake, and then run away."

"Duffy!" Amy exclaimed in horror. "That's crazy! Why would anyone do such a horrible thing?"

"That's ridiculous," Cynthia agreed. "It's just your fever talking. The nurse said it was up again. You have to stop this, Duffy: hating the hospital, not letting yourself feel safe here. It's keeping you from getting well. You have to relax."

Duffy made a rude sound. "Relax? Are you crazy? How can I relax?"

"Maybe what happened," Cynthia proposed calmly, "is, a student nurse came along and intended to take you inside. She released the brake, and then something caught her attention . . . another patient needing something . . . and she forgot she'd released the brake. I'll ask around, okay? Will that make you feel better?"

Duffy felt tears of frustration threatening again. And she realized then what felt so wrong about the way people were reacting: They were all so sure the chair's race down the hill had been an accident. How could they be so sure? How *could* they?

She wasn't.

Frustrated and feeling extremely ill, she muttered, "You won't get any answers from anyone, Cynthia. Smith didn't when he asked about the sign on the elevator door. No one will admit to releasing that brake. Forget it."

Her parents arrived then. She could tell by the look on her mother's face that they had already heard about the runaway chair. Maybe now they'd take her home.

Amy gestured to Cynthia that they should leave. "We'll come back later," she told Duffy. "You'll be feeling better then."

That was Amy. Always looking on the bright side.

Was there a bright side?

The only bright side, it seemed to her, was that her parents might take her home now, agreeing that she wasn't safe here.

That idea was quickly squelched. While her parents were upset about the downhill race, they were not only convinced that it had been an "unfortunate accident," but their total faith in Twelvetrees Community Hospital and Dr. Jonas Morgan remained unshaken. If they had a concern, it seemed to be that their very imaginative daughter might be overreacting.

"Honey, you have to calm down," her mother said. "Although," she added, "I do think someone could have stayed with you out on that slope. It's so steep."

And her father said, "Duffy, of *course* it was an accident. What else could it be? You wouldn't be reacting this way if you weren't so sick."

When they had gone and Duffy was waiting for Jane to arrive, she tried to tell herself her parents were right. It had simply been an accident.

Because she couldn't think of a single thing she had ever done to anyone that would make them deliberately send her flying down a steep hill, trapped in a wheelchair. So if there was no reason, there was no plot to kill her. It had been an accident, period.

But . . . she felt the wind again ripping at her face, felt the horror of being trapped in the speeding chair, saw the icy waters of the lake approaching . . . and heard again, as clearly as if she were once again out on the top of that hill, the sound of stealthy footsteps approaching behind her, the creak of the brake being released.

Accident?

How could she be sure?

She wasn't sure of anything anymore.

Chapter 9

Duffy missed Kit fiercely. Images of the two of them exploring the woods, Kit with his ever-present camera, she with a stick in hand, played across the dingy white walls of her room. Being with Kit had always been so easy. He never demanded brilliant conversation or her complete attention, didn't get his feelings hurt if she sat down on a log and became engrossed in a book while he wandered around taking pictures, and he always seemed to understand when she was in what her mother called "one of your moods, Duffy."

Where was he now? He couldn't have reached the coast yet. She tried to picture a map of the United States in her mind. Where would Kit be by now? Didn't you have to go across the desert to reach California? What if that old rattletrap of his broke down?

A flash of anger at Kit darted through her consciousness. He should be *here* now. She needed him. He'd always been there before. Couldn't he have put up with that awful uncle of his for just one more week?

Ashamed of her selfishness, a wave of nausea flooded over her.

But even when the shame eased, the nausea didn't. And her head had begun to ache, a new symptom. Was the flu finally attacking her full force?

As she struggled to pull herself to a sitting position, she noticed something odd about the ceiling light. It seemed surrounded by a frothy halo, something she had never noticed before. Were all fluorescent lights like that, or had the flu suddenly attacked her eyesight as well as her stomach and her head?

She felt much worse than she had when she had first arrived at Twelvetrees Community Hospital.

"This is not the place to come when you want to get well," she told the aide who brought her dinner. "I didn't feel this rotten when I first came in here."

"You're just having a bad day," the aide said matter-of-factly. "If I were you, I'd consider myself lucky to be alive. Smith Lewis said he couldn't believe you survived that race down the hill. And you without a scratch! It's a miracle."

That sentiment was echoed a while later by the nurse who came in to take Duffy's temperature again and dispense more pills. "You should count your blessings," she said. "Surviving such an escapade — it's incredible. You're a very lucky girl, Dorothy."

"Yeah, right," Duffy said harshly. Then she added slyly, "Since you admit I'm having a bad day, how about making it better by letting me take a shower before visiting hours? Please? Just one tiny little shower?" A shower would definitely calm her down and ease the queasiness in her stomach.

"Absolutely not!"

Duffy groaned.

"Someone would have to go with you and no one has time. And didn't you just say your stomach was upset? Why on earth would you want to get out of bed and walk all the way down the hall when you're feeling so crummy?"

"Because maybe if I had a shower, I wouldn't *feel* so crummy," Duffy retorted. "God, I hate this place!"

Amy and Cynthia stopped in briefly when they were collecting the dinner trays.

Duffy thought Cynthia looked beat, and said so.

"Yeah, I guess I am," Cynthia admitted. "I keep falling asleep at night when I should be studying. But no school tomorrow . . . teachers' conference, so I figured I could afford to work today. They're awfully busy here."

"I know," Duffy said grimly. "They won't let me take a shower because they think I need a keeper and everyone's too busy to go with me. I think maybe I'll just take one, anyway."

Amy gave her a warning glance. "Duffy, honestly, why can't you just obey the rules for a change?" Sighing, she turned her attention to Cynthia. "You work too hard," she said softly. "What you need is a man in your life. Someone to take you to a funny movie or out dancing, help you unwind a little."

"I don't have time to date," Cynthia said.

"Well, *I* do," Amy said, her mouth curving downward. "For all the good it does me." For a brief moment, her round face filled with sadness. "I thought that Dylan and I . . ." Then, just as quickly, her face cleared and her usual cheerful expression returned. "Oh, well, that's life, right, Duff?"

"Right." But Duffy was surprised by the momentary bleakness in Amy's face. Dylan had told everyone that his split with Amy was "mutual," meaning, Duffy thought, that they'd both decided it was time to split up. But it certainly didn't seem as if Amy was happy about the decision.

After Amy and Cynthia had taken her tray and left, Duffy began to wonder. Had Dylan been lying about his breakup with Amy? Maybe to protect her from embarrassment? That was the kind of thing Dylan would do. He didn't like hurting people. But Amy seemed hurt, anyway.

Duffy felt briefly ashamed, because she had often wondered what outgoing, popular Dylan saw in a girl who got upset if her library books were one day overdue. Knowing now what a nice, thoughtful person Amy was didn't ease Duffy's discomfort. And remembering how attentive Dylan had been since she'd become a patient didn't help. She wondered nervously if she had, innocently enough, had anything to do with Dylan and Amy's breakup. She hoped not. She would hate that.

It was silly to think about stuff like that now, Duffy reminded herself. Right now, all she wanted was to feel better. And despite what everyone said, Duffy knew that a soothing, hot shower would help.

After all, it hadn't actually been the shower the nurse had objected to. Only the need for someone to accompany Duffy.

Well, I don't *need* any help, she thought, preparing to slide out of bed. I can take a shower all by myself. I've been doing it for years.

The room spun wildly. She saw double, and her knees melted. Her stomach heaved. "Oboy," she murmured, clutching her stomach. This was not going to be easy.

Kit always said nothing worth doing was easy. And he should know. Nothing had ever been easy for him.

Duffy managed to slide her feet into her slippers, although looking down she saw four feet instead of two. The room spun crazily as she slipped into her robe and stood up straight. But although she teetered dangerously, she remained upright.

"Great!" she whispered, and collected her shampoo, razor, soap, washcloth, and towel from the cabinet in her bedside table, Then, walking very carefully, she made her way to the door and peered out.

It was still very early evening, that quiet time after dinner when patients often nap before visiting hours. The halls were empty, the nurses away from the station, eating their own dinner or busy dispensing medication in other rooms.

Duffy decided to risk it. Maybe she'd get lucky.

She did. Clutching the wall for support, she made it to the twin shower rooms at the end of the hall without being stopped. The first door was locked, but the second doorknob turned easily in her hand. Heaving a deep sigh of relief, Duffy slipped inside and flipped on the ceiling light, locking the door of the small, beige cubicle behind her.

She noticed with mild curiosity that this light, too, had a strange halo. Her head pounded anew, and her stomach did a dizzying dance. But there was the shower stall, so inviting in spite of the ugliness of the grim little room. A shower would make her feel better. Probably do more good than a thousand little pills.

The shower felt unbelievably good, like a drink of water after a long desert trek. The tension in her muscles melted away under the flow of the wonderfully hot water. Her skin responded with joy, and Duffy felt momentarily well enough to hum a tune as she lathered and rinsed. Still dizzy, she was careful to lean against the cold, clammy tile as she scrubbed.

She had just finished wrapping her blissfully clean hair in the towel and was in the process of awkwardly shaving her legs in the narrow tiled cubicle when she felt a sudden blast of cold air against her shoulders. She paused, lifting her head to listen.

Had the door opened? No, that couldn't be. She clearly remembered locking it.

As she straightened up, there was the click of a light switch and the room disappeared into a thick cloak of darkness.

Duffy was standing, soaking wet, in total, silent blackness.

Chapter 10

Duffy's first clear thought as she stood, wet and disbelieving in the shower stall, was that there had been a power failure. Cynthia had warned her that such failures were frequent occurrences in the old building.

But . . . that wouldn't explain why the door had opened, admitting that wave of cool air over the top of the glass shower door . . . or the sound of the light switch being flicked off.

How could the door have opened? She hadn't heard the sound of a key turning in the lock.

But the water had been running the whole time. The sound of someone turning a key would have been muffled.

Was there someone in the room with her now?

Beginning to tremble, Duffy listened, not breathing. She heard nothing. Not a sound.

With her only towel wrapped, turban-style around her wet hair, she grabbed her robe from the top of the shower door and threw it on over her water-slicked skin. Then, anxious to leave the musty, pitch-black room, she turned to retrieve her shower supplies from the tiled ledge.

Suddenly, the shower door latch clicked open behind her. With only enough time to gasp in shock, Duffy was seized from behind and thrown bodily, facedown, onto the floor of the stall, where several inches of water had puddled due to the slow drain.

Warm, soapy water filled her mouth and nose. She choked, gagged, spat, and struggled to pull herself upright, out of the foamy water. But a knee in her back pinned her down, rendering her immobile.

What . . . what was happening?

She was too tall for the tiny space. Her legs, cruelly bent at the knee, were crumpled up against the cold, wet tile. A fist pressed down painfully on the back of her neck. She was completely helpless, her mouth and nose submerged in warm water, unable to move . . . to scream . . . to make a sound . . . unable to cry out for the help she needed.

Her mind, stunned and shaken, reeled in an effort to think clearly. All it could manage was a shocked, terrified, *What is happening?*

But as she struggled desperately to free herself of the deadening weight on her back, to lift her head out of the soapy water, her mind cleared, and began to race frantically.

I can't breathe. I will drown in this tiny little bit of water if I don't do something . . . something. But what? What can I do?

Then she realized that her razor was still clutched in her right hand. A small pink plastic grooming tool, she was afraid it could do no harm to her attacker. It was designed specifically *not* to do harm.

But it was all she had.

Desperate, she slashed backward, hard.

A harsh, guttural scream of pain echoed in the stall . . . a whispered curse . . . the fist left the back of her neck.

Duffy threw her head up out of the water, gasping for air.

The whispered, angry cursing above her continued as bright red droplets of blood began plopping into the soapy puddle surrounding her.

The little pink razor had come through for her.

Duffy lay in fear, her head stiffly held up out of the water at an awkward, painful angle. Had her desperate slash made her attacker angrier with her? Would the next attack, when it came, be even more vicious? She had no strength left to fight . . . how could she hold her head up out of the water if another attack came?

She waited . . . not breathing . . . her heart beating wildly against her chest, tears of terror stinging her eyelids.

With one final, whispered curse, the weight left her back. Another whiff of cool air entered the stall as the shower door was flung open.

And then came the blessed, beautiful sound of the wooden door to the room opening and ferociously slamming shut.

She was alone again.

But someone was very, very angry with her.

Duffy lay on the floor of the stall, sobbing tears

of fear and relief for what seemed like a long, long time, cradling her head on her arm to keep it up out of the water.

When she felt her legs going numb, she used the palms of her hands pressed against the clammy tile to pull herself to her feet. Unsteady, her head screaming in pain, her stomach lurching, she swayed and had to lean against the wall for support.

Her white robe was soaking wet. The towel wrapped around her head had been dislodged in the struggle; cold strands of sodden hair chilled the back of her neck.

She began trembling violently and although she tried to still her shaking limbs, nearly biting through her lower lip with the effort, her body refused to obey her.

It was so dark . . . so dark and damp. . . .

Taking a deep breath, she slowly pushed open the glass shower door, peering into the velvety darkness for any sign of a threat.

What if her attacker hadn't really left? Suppose it was a trick — slamming the door shut to make it seem as if Duffy were safely alone? Suppose he was hiding, there in the darkness, waiting for her to emerge from the shower stall?

Her bones paralyzed with fear, Duffy listened anxiously.

But the tiny room was utterly still. No sound of angry breathing broke the silence.

Finally sure that she really was alone, Duffy emerged from the stall, still shaking and unsteady, and moved toward the door.

If she could make it to the door, pull it open, step out into the hall, away from the horrid musty smell, the chilly dampness, the unbroken darkness, she would be all right. She *would*. The shaking would stop and someone would come to help her. She would be safe again.

Wouldn't she?

But the minute she stepped out into the dimly lighted corridor, she was blinded by the strange halos around the overhead lights. Shielding her eyes with her hands, she sagged against the wall. The full horror of what had happened to her flooded over her in an enormous wave, nearly knocking her off her feet.

This time there was no question of an *accident*. Someone had tried to kill her. She didn't know who, or why she only knew that they had.

And they had almost succeeded.

Chapter 11

There was no one in Duffy's end of the corridor, but she could see white uniforms scurrying about in the distance.

"Help," she whispered, shaking violently. "Somebody please help me."

No one heard or noticed her.

She raised her voice. "*Help* me!" It stunned her that people in the hospital could continue to go about their business as usual, after what had happened to her. Couldn't they see? Couldn't they tell? Why didn't someone rush to her aid?

And then hysteria took over. Completely losing control, Duffy opened her mouth and a scream came out. "Help, help!" she cried and lurched away from the wall, breaking into a staggering run. Still screaming, she moved down the hall, hands against the walls for support.

And the white figures in the distance stopped what they were doing to stare at her.

Her sodden robe hung open, her damp hair hung limply against her face, her bare feet slipped and slid on the cold tile as she staggered on. "Help me!" she sobbed, her voice hoarse with fear, "somebody help me!"

At the other end of the hall, Smith Lewis broke into a run.

When he reached her, she fell against him, gasping, still shaking violently.

"Help," she whispered, "please." And then, giving in, she slumped against him and her eyes closed.

When Duffy awoke, she was lying in her bed, covered with a sheet. She was surrounded by two nurses, Smith Lewis, Dr. Morgan, and Amy Severn. Smith and Amy looked worried. The older nurse was removing a blood pressure cuff, the younger one holding out a tiny paper cup, and the doctor was frowning down at his patient.

It took Duffy a few moments to remember exactly why they were all staring down at her. When the shower scene returned, in full graphic detail, she gasped and began moaning softly, "Nononono. . . ."

Smith was the first to speak. "What, Duffy? What happened?"

Duffy closed her eyes. "Someone . . . someone tried to kill me," she whispered. "In the shower . . ."

When she opened her eyes, what she saw shocked her. There was total disbelief in every face peering down at her.

The two nurses exchanged a glance that clearly

said, "delirium." Smith and Amy looked doubtful, and the doctor regarded his patient as he might a lab specimen, gazing down at her with detached curiosity.

"I've checked you over thoroughly," he told her, "and aside from some nasty bumps that are probably going to turn black-and-blue on your back and neck, you're okay. Took a bad fall, did you?"

"I . . . no, I didn't fall," she managed. "I didn't. Someone . . . I was attacked. In the shower . . ."

"Attacked? In the shower?" the older nurse repeated, in the same way that she might have said, "You say you have a fairy godmother at home?"

Duffy clenched her teeth. She had never expected that she wouldn't be believed. Not this time. Would she look the way she did if she hadn't been attacked? Couldn't they see?

"I know it sounds crazy," she cried. "But I'm telling you the truth! I was taking a shower and someone came in and knocked me down on the floor and sat on my back and wouldn't let me go, and there was water in the bottom of the shower and I almost drowned . . ." She stopped. She had never faced such disbelief in her life.

And that terrified her. If she couldn't convince anyone she was telling the truth, who would help her? What if the attacker wasn't finished with her? She needed someone on her side.

"You've got to believe me!" Duffy struggled to sit up in bed, but she was too weak, too nauseated. Sinking back against the pillow, she tried again.

"Please, it *did* happen. I wouldn't make up something so crazy." Her eyes appealed to Amy. "Amy? You believe me, don't you?"

Amy flushed and took a step backward.

"Of course you wouldn't make up such a story," the older nurse said soothingly. "It's the fever, dear. This kind of thing happens all the time, doesn't it, doctor?" As she turned away, Duffy heard her mutter under her breath, "Shouldn't have taken her off the IV. Too soon."

"I didn't *imagine* it!" Duffy shouted, her eyes flying from face to face in a search for understanding. "I was in the shower, and the door opened, and the light went off . . ." Tears of frustration spilled from her eyes.

"Didn't you lock the door?" the ponytailed nurse asked gently. "My goodness, Duffy, you should always lock the door."

"Of *course* I locked the door," Duffy protested. "I did! I locked it! I *remember* locking it."

"Well, there you are," the older nurse said cheerfully. "If you locked the door, how could anyone possibly have gotten in?" She smiled. "I don't think anyone around here can walk through walls, Dorothy."

Duffy wanted to scream. "Don't talk to me as if I'm two years old," she sobbed angrily. "I *did* lock the stupid door and someone got in anyway. They must have had a key."

"Wait one sec," the young nurse said, and disappeared. As promised, she was back immediately, a round metal ring of keys in her hand. "See, Duffy?"

she said, holding up the ring. "This is the only extra key we have to that shower room. And it's right here, on the ring where it belongs. And the ring was hanging behind the nurses' station, right where it's supposed to be. So . . ."

"So, nothing!" Duffy snapped, swiping at her tears with the back of her hand. "Someone must have taken it, used it, and then put it back. Let me see it."

"I would have seen someone taking it," the nurse said defensively. But she handed Duffy the ring.

"Which key is it?"

The nurse pointed.

"Dr. Morgan, Dr. Morgan, to ICU, stat!" a voice barked over the PA system.

The doctor patted Duffy's hair awkwardly, handed the older nurse Duffy's chart, told the patient to "Relax and take it easy," gave the nurse medication orders for Duffy, and left.

Ignoring his departure because it was clear he wouldn't have believed her, Duffy continued to study the key. It hung on a leather thong. "Look," she said, pointing, "there's a smear on the strap. It's probably blood. I slashed at the person who attacked me and I know I hurt him because there was blood in the water. See?" Pointing, she held up the key ring.

Smith and the younger nurse examined it, while Amy hung back, an expression of revulsion on her face.

"Oh, Duffy, I don't think that stain is new," the nurse exclaimed. "I'm sure I remember seeing it before. I thinks it's paint, from when they painted behind the nurses' station."

Duffy could see then that it was hopeless. The nurses, scolding her for taking a shower alone against orders, clearly thought that she had been hallucinating. Amy was looking at her with cow-eyed sympathy, and Smith was chewing thoughtfully on his lower lip.

Not a single one of them believed the attack had actually taken place.

If no one believed her . . . who would *help* her? She knew now that someone, for some crazy reason, was angry with her, wanted to hurt her, kill her. As insane as that sounded, she knew it was true.

Duffy was startled by a sudden pinprick in her upper left arm.

"Doctor ordered a sedative for you," the older nurse said. "It'll calm you down. My, you really let your imagination get the best of you, didn't you? That's not wise, Dorothy. Not in your condition."

Duffy flopped angrily over on her side and burrowed beneath the blanket, before anyone could see her helpless, frightened tears.

Chapter 12

Duffy was floating somewhere in that blissful haven between sleep and reality when she heard her father's voice.

"Look, if my daughter says she was attacked in the shower, then that's what happened." He sounded angry and very, very far away. But he had to be out in the hall. "She doesn't tell lies."

Sure, I do, Daddy, Duffy thought woozily. I lied that time I didn't get home until three in the morning and you were waiting up. My date didn't have a flat tire. I just didn't want to leave the party. Sorry, Daddy.

"Nobody said anything about lying, Mr. Quinn," Dr. Morgan's voice replied, also from a distance. Both voices sounded as if they were coming from behind a giant wall of cotton. "Your daughter had a bad fall, that's our theory, and the bump on the head, combined with her illness, caused her to hallucinate. It's not all that unusual."

A third voice joined them . . . the gray-haired nurse. "We did have Security check the shower room, of course. There was no sign of forced entry."

She tried to sit up in bed and call her father, but she toppled sideways immediately. She was floating in a sea of clouds. It was not an unpleasant sensation.

"We want to see her," her mother's voice said.

"I'm sorry," Dr. Morgan answered from his faraway place, "but I'd rather you didn't. I gave her a sedative. Let her sleep. She's had a rough time of it. Since tomorrow is a holiday, we've added morning visiting hours. You can see Duffy then."

What? No visiting hours tonight? Well, that certainly wasn't fair. Not the least bit. It wasn't *her* fault she'd had a rough time of it. Why were they punishing her by stealing her visiting hours?

And then her head fell back on the pillow, her eyes shut, and she disappeared into a thick, drugged sleep.

When she awoke sometime later, her room was still shrouded in darkness broken only by the faint glow of the small night-light by her door. She hated the darkness. She would never feel safe in the dark again.

Her head pounded, her stomach rode a carousel. But she was no longer lost in that drug-induced twilight zone.

The entire fourth floor was shrouded in silence. There were no quiet, rubber-soled footsteps out in the hall, no clattering of gurney wheels, no hushed conversation between nurses and orderlies, no clanking of metal rings on curtain slides. The hospital was as still and silent as . . . death.

Death . . . she had come so close, so close, in that shower stall. Duffy pulled the sheet up around her neck, clutching its hem with her fists. No one believed her. They all thought she was crazy or delirious. But it *had* happened. She remembered every single horrible second of it and as the memories returned, her heart began pounding.

Why would someone want to kill her?

Why had she been sent racing down that steep hill toward the lake? Why had she been attacked in the shower stall? And the elevator . . . had the out-of-order sign really been switched accidentally? Or had it been done on purpose, by someone who knew she was planning to go downstairs to the gift shop?

She couldn't remember who knew she had planned to leave her room to go downstairs. How many people had she told? Hadn't she announced it, loud and clear? And anyone she'd told could have told half a dozen other people. There were no secrets in this place. The whole hospital probably knew she planned to go for a walk, knew she was headed for the showers.

Duffy's head pounded, and her skin, dry and parched, burned with fever.

I really *am* sick, she silently told the cracked ceiling.

But am I sick enough to imagine a vicious attack?

Was the nurse right? Could being this sick make a person imagine all kinds of horrible things?

No . . . she was positive someone was trying to kill her. She couldn't have imagined the terrible scene in the shower.

Or . . . could she?

And no one had believed her. They were all so sure her life hadn't really been in danger. How could they *all* be wrong? How could she be the only person who was right?

Smith's dark head appeared in her doorway. "Just checking," he said as he moved toward her bed. "I see you're awake. Feeling better?"

Smith planned to be a doctor. Someone had said he read a lot of medical books. Maybe he could answer the question that was racing around in her mind. She would rather ask Dylan, but Dylan wasn't around.

"Smith," she began as he stood over her, looking down, "could a really high fever make a person imagine the kind of thing that happened to me today? I mean, it seemed so *real*. The light going out, the door to the shower stall opening, being pushed to the floor, the knee in my back . . . I know I have bruises to prove it. I can feel them."

Without waiting for an invitation, Smith sat, carefully, on the edge of her bed. "Let's look at it logically," he said. "Made anyone mad enough to want to wipe you off the planet?"

"No, of course not! I mean, I know I'm not the world's best patient . . ."

Smith laughed. "Boy, is that an understatement! But I've seen worse patients and as far as I know, no one ever attacked any of them in the shower. So . . . unless you can come up with a logical reason why someone would want to get rid of you, I guess the answer to your question is yes, a high fever *can* make you think all kinds of things."

That wasn't the answer Duffy wanted. "But my bruises . . ." she protested.

Smith shrugged. "Doc Morgan's probably right. You must have fallen. Knocking up against ceramic tile could turn anyone's skin black and blue."

He didn't believe the attack had really happened.

Kit would have. Kit would have believed her. And then he would have helped her figure out *why* it had happened.

But Kit wasn't there.

"Look," Smith offered, "if it'll make you feel better, I'll camp outside your door tonight. I'm off tomorrow so I can sleep late. I'll park a chair there and read, okay?"

No, not okay. Because he didn't *believe* her. He was just humoring her, as if she were a psychiatric patient up on the fifth floor. "Don't do me any favors," she said haughtily, turning her back on him. "Since you're so sure it's just my fevered little mind attacking me, I don't see why you'd think I need protection. Just go away, please. Leave me and my feeble brain in peace, okay?"

"C'mon, Duffy," he said in exasperation, "you *asked*! I just told you what I thought."

"Go away," she repeated stubbornly.

With a heavy sigh of resignation, he turned and left the room.

Duffy was overcome with nausea, attacking her

in huge waves. She fought it successfully and when it had passed, she thought about what Smith and the others had said. She wished she could believe their theory, and accept it. Wouldn't that make her feel better, if the whole horrible thing had been unreal?

Well, if they were right, there was no reason why she couldn't try to relax and get some sleep. That would make morning come faster and another miserable night in this awful place would be behind her.

She was just drifting off when she heard voices again, outside in the hall directly beyond her door, which stood slightly ajar.

"I don't know, doctor. I haven't seen it."

Duffy recognized the voice. The young ponytailed nurse.

"I was just going off duty, doctor, but if you want me to look for it, of course I'll be happy to."

Then a deeper voice, unfamiliar. "You do that. I don't care if it takes all night, I want that bottle found. In the meantime, if any of the patients start complaining about nausea or dizziness or happen to mention visual problems, for instance that the lights look funny, pay attention. It could mean we've found our missing digoxin." The voice deepened, became harsher. "You'd better hope and pray that medication wasn't given to the wrong patient, because I'm holding you accountable."

Duffy, listening intently, heard the threat of tears in the young nurse's voice as she replied shakily, "Yes, doctor, I'll start looking right this minute. I'll let you know when I find it."

There was no answer, only the sound of muffled, angry footsteps striding away.

Duffy lay unmoving in her bed, staring up at the ceiling. Nausea? Dizziness? Lights looking funny?

Those were *her* symptoms.

Chapter 13

Duffy huddled under the blankets, a paralyzed lump. Digoxin? That wasn't the name of her antibiotic. She had asked. Hers was "something-myocin." But the unseen doctor had just described, perfectly, the way she was feeling. He had said a medication was missing . . . that it wasn't where it was supposed to be.

That was scary.

Duffy chewed on her lower lip. Even if that medicine *was* missing, how could that have anything to do with her? Nobody had given her anything new or strange. Just the capsules.

The capsules . . . could someone have mixed them up with the missing medication? Given her the wrong kind of pills? Did the missing digoxin come in the same kind of pill as her something-myocin?

Anyone could make a mistake. Even in a hospital. After all, she already knew they'd lost the medication in the first place.

But . . . what if . . . what if it wasn't a mistake? If given to the wrong patient, could those missing pills *kill* someone? Cynthia had said the reason they had to be so careful with the charts was that any mix-up could lead to the wrong medication being dispensed. And she had said that the wrong medication could sometimes result in . . . *death*.

If someone really were trying to kill her, wouldn't that be the perfect way? Would anyone even question her death?

No, they probably wouldn't. They'd blame it on her fever.

Her mouth set grimly, Duffy grabbed the call button and pressed on it, not releasing her hold until she heard soft footsteps approaching her door.

Amy Severn, looking anxious, came into the room. "What's wrong, Duffy?"

"What are you still doing here?" Duffy asked with surprise as the Junior Volunteer hurried to her bedside. "It must be after midnight."

"It is. Two of the nurses have the flu and none of the volunteers wanted to help out tonight. So I said I would." Amy sighed heavily. "Cynthia and Smith and Dylan all work nights sometimes. I don't know how they do it. I'm beat! We've had two emergencies already, and old Mrs. Creole is giving us fits. That woman is the *worst* patient on this earth. She makes you look like a saint!" Another sigh. "At least I can sleep in tomorrow."

Ignoring that, Duffy asked, "Amy, have you heard anything about any missing medication? I overheard one of the doctors talking . . ."

"Oh, Duffy, the patients aren't supposed to know anything about that. As if we didn't have enough problems tonight, Dr. Brooks has everyone scrambling, hunting for a missing bottle of digoxin. He's really upset that we can't find it."

"What's it for? The digoxin."

"Heart."

"What does it look like? Not the bottle, the medicine."

"Capsules. I think the bottle they're looking for was part of the inventory in Mr. Latham's room, and now they can't find it."

"Who's Mr. Latham?"

"A patient. He died. Duffy, is this why you called me in here? We're awfully busy."

Amy turned to leave, but Duffy stopped her. "Wait, Amy! I'm not just asking out of nosiness. I heard the doctor talking about the side effects of that medication. And I have *all* of them."

Skepticism showed on Amy's face.

"I do," Duffy insisted. "Really. They started right after the nurse gave me the first capsules, when they took my IV out. My stomach's upset, I'm dizzy . . . and I heard him say something about the lights looking strange. Well, when I look at the lights, I see weird little halos. They were never there before."

"Duffy . . ." Amy's voice was weary. "There's no way your medication could have been mixed up with that digoxin."

"But you're not *sure* that it didn't get mixed up, are you?" Duffy pressed relentlessly. "And if it did, you don't know what it would do, do you?"

Amy shook her head. "No . . . I haven't read as

much about medications as Cynthia and Dylan and Smith. You should ask one of them."

"I want you to have my medicine checked out. Make sure they're not giving me that missing heart stuff by mistake, okay? You can do that, can't you?" Duffy knew how neurotic she sounded, how paranoid. She couldn't help it. Amy had to realize how important this was.

The weariness in Amy's voice was replaced by annoyance. That surprised Duffy. She didn't know Amy ever got annoyed. "Duffy, really, I wish you'd quit worrying. The nurses are very careful with medications. They don't screw up on something that important."

Duffy pounced. "They lost a whole bottle of medication, didn't they?"

Amy shrugged. "People lose things all the time. The bottle will turn up. It's not as if some nurse made a mistake and gave the digoxin to the wrong patient. It's just misplaced, that's all."

Duffy's voice rose as she fought panic. Amy *had* to listen to her. "You don't *know* the wrong patient isn't getting that missing medicine. I'm telling you I have all the symptoms the doctor was describing, and I want you to check my medication to make sure I'm not being given that digoxin stuff by mistake." Out of desperation, her voice hardened. "You wouldn't want my parents suing this hospital because you didn't do your duty, would you? The hospital board wouldn't like that at all. They'd blame *you*."

Amy's face crumpled in dismay and then, for the

first time since Duffy had known her, she lost her temper. "You're being hateful, Duffy Quinn!" she whispered in a hushed, angry voice. "People are just so sick and tired of you making such a fuss all the time. Why can't you be like other patients and sleep? You'd get better faster. Then you could go home and we'd *all* be happy!"

Amy's voice rose as Duffy, her mouth open, stared in astonishment. "I am sick and tired of being nice to you when you don't care a thing about how *I'm* feeling! I don't know what Dylan sees in you, why he would dump me for you — " Her voice broke and, near tears, she turned on her heel and rushed out of the room.

Duffy's nausea returned, turning her stomach into a seesaw. Feeling sick and abandoned, she buried her head in her pillow, moaning.

If Amy — quiet, gentle Amy, who always listened and who always seemed interested — didn't believe her, no one would. No one.

She was alone.

Did Amy really think Dylan had "dumped" her for Duffy?

Oh, God, I am so sick, she cried silently, self-pity overcoming her and wiping out thoughts of Dylan and Amy. She was nauseated and headachey and dizzy. Terror suddenly struck Duffy like a sledgehammer . . . could she be dying? Was this what dying felt like? Was she right about someone deliberately giving her the digoxin, and now it was killing her?

If the digoxin had been in the capsules all along,

ever since Duffy started taking them, she'd had more than a dose or two.

How much of that stuff would it take to kill someone?

She wasn't taking any more of them. If no one would listen to her and have the medicine checked out, she wasn't going to let another capsule pass her lips. She didn't care *how* mad the nurses got. Let them kick her out of the hospital if they wanted to. It would probably be the best thing that could happen to her.

Duffy lay awake all night, fighting nausea and fever, huddled deep in her covers.

Several times, panic overtook her and her hands flew to the call button. Then, remembering with bitter disappointment Amy's disbelief, she let the call button drop into the sheet folds. What was the use?

They all thought she was hysterical . . . or crazy . . . or delirious . . . or all three.

It was hopeless.

She had to find a way to prove the digoxin was in her capsules. First thing in the morning . . .

But morning seemed very far away.

Chapter 14

Frightened by how sick she was feeling, Duffy appealed to her doctor the following morning.

She knew there was no point in sharing her suspicions with him. He wouldn't believe that someone had switched her antibiotic with the missing digoxin any more than Amy had. She would have to try a different tack.

"I think the new pills are making me sick," she said as he glanced at her chart. "I feel sicker than I did when I came in here. Maybe I'm allergic to them. You'd better give me something else."

Dr. Morgan tugged at his earring and frowned. "That's just the drug fighting your infection," he said brusquely. "There's a war being fought in your system and I guarantee the medication is winning. We're pretty sure you've got the flu. The blood tests rule out anything more serious. You'll feel like new in a day or two. Just hang in there, okay?"

And without waiting for an answer from Duffy as to whether or not she was willing to "hang in there," he left.

"Those pills are making me sick!" she cried after him, but it was hopeless. He wasn't listening.

No one was listening. Where Duffy Quinn's fears were concerned, the whole world had gone stone-deaf.

The ceiling light blinked down at her coldly, its strange little halo reminding her that there was something very wrong with her "system" and it wasn't a war being waged by an antibiotic. There *was* no antibiotic in her system. She was convinced there was only digoxin.

A clattering sound out in the hallway preceded Smith's curly head appearing in the doorway.

Something about the sound made Duffy tilt her head and listen carefully. It was probably just one of hundreds of ordinary hospital noises, but . . .

"How's it going?" Smith inquired, leaning against the doorframe. "You recovered from the heebie-jeebies?"

"Go away," she said rudely. "I don't want to talk to people who think I'm crazy."

"Hey," he said, moving into the room, "I never said that. You're sick, that's all. You'd be surprised by some of the stories we hear from patients on heavy doses of medication. I know you *think* what happened was real, but — "

"It *was* real," Duffy said, but her voice lacked conviction. She had tried during the night, throughout the long, sleepless hours, to think of a reason why someone would want to harm her, and she'd failed.

That was the biggest stumbling block to believing

and accepting that someone was deliberately trying to hurt, even kill her. Didn't the police always look for a motive? Wasn't that the most important thing? The "why" of a crime? And there *wasn't* any "why" here.

So, unless there was a crazed psychotic killer in the hospital, one of those weirdos who didn't need a reason to commit murder, there shouldn't be anyone after her.

Maybe Smith and all the others were right. Maybe it *was* the fever.

She would try not to think about it. No point in making herself even crazier when no one was willing to listen. They'd whisk her off to a padded room if she wasn't careful.

But she was still going to find a way to check what was really in her capsules. She didn't know how yet, but —

"What was that noise out in the hall?" she asked Smith. "That rattling sound. What was it?"

"Oh, that. A gurney. One of its wheels is loose. Dylan was supposed to fix it, but . . ."

"A gurney? One of those rolling tables?"

Smith nodded. "Yeah. Taking it downstairs. To the morgue. Why?" He said "morgue" as easily as he might have said "mall."

Duffy shuddered. The morgue. Where they kept the patients who had . . . died. Had someone planned to send her there yesterday?

"Why?" Smith repeated. "Why do you want to know what the noise was?"

She shook her head. "Oh, it's just . . ." Her voice drifted off. She was positive that the sound was identical to the last noise she'd heard that night.

Why would someone be moving a gurney out of her room? Why had it been there in the first place?

"It's just that I heard that sound the other night," she said thoughtfully. "In my room, I think . . ."

His reaction was the same as Dylan's had been when Duffy recognized the soft *slap-slap* of rubber-soled shoes. "Yeah? Well, the hospital is full of them, Duffy. It would be weird if you *hadn't* heard that noise before."

"Yes, but . . ." Oh, what was the use? Trying to explain was a waste of time. "Forget it."

Had she learned anything new? Anything helpful?

The gurneys were used sometimes to take patients who had died down to the basement morgue.

Did that mean anything?

"What are you thinking about?" Smith asked, his eyes on her face.

"Nothing." Why had that gurney been in her room? If two people had been fooling around, as Jane suggested, they wouldn't have needed a gurney. They had the bed.

Could the rickety old gurney have been outside in the hall and not in her room at all?

Maybe. Sound carried better late at night when the hospital was quiet. Maybe the gurney had been out in the hall, passing by her room.

But it sounded closer than that . . .

If she'd heard it at all. How could she be sure? She couldn't.

"You've got that look on your face," Smith said, snapping her back to attention. "You're thinking weird things again, I can tell."

"Did . . . did anybody die a couple of nights ago? The night everyone tells me was just a bad dream?"

Smith sighed and shook his head. "No, Duffy, no one died. We had a couple of emergencies, just like we always do at night, but everyone pulled through just fine. If you did hear a gurney, it was probably bringing a post-op patient back up from surgery. Or maybe someone was just being moved to another floor."

No one had died that night.

Then she remembered something Amy had said, about someone dying recently. The man with the missing digoxin . . .

"What about Mr. Latham? Amy said he'd died. When was that?"

Smith tilted his head, thinking. "Old Man Latham? Pillar of the community, member of the hospital board . . . I'm not sure exactly when he died. Couple of days ago, I guess. Just before you got here. I wasn't on duty that night. Everyone was freaked out the next day, though. The old guy had donated mega-bucks to the hospital. Had a bad ticker, I heard."

Latham had died before Duffy was admitted. So his death couldn't possibly have anything to do with what was happening to her. Not that she had really thought it did. She hadn't even *known* the man.

After admonishing her to "get some sleep, you look awful, Duffy," Smith left.

When he had disappeared through the open door, a depressed Duffy rolled over on her side and stared out the window. As she turned, the sheets coiled around her legs, imprisoning her. Panicking momentarily, she began kicking out, desperate to be free of the scratchy cocoon.

"What on earth . . ." Cynthia cried as she entered the room and found Duffy wrestling with her bedding. "Duffy, what are you *doing*?" Then she added more quietly to Jane, who was directly behind her, "Oh, Lord, she's lost it! I knew this was coming!" and ran over to grab Duffy's wrists.

"Leave me alone!" Duffy shouted, her face scarlet. "I'm just tangled, that's all." She yanked the last bit of sheet away from her bare legs. Glaring up at the blue-uniformed Cynthia, she asked caustically, "Did you really think I was losing it? Did my doctor warn you to watch out for weird behavior in room 417?"

When Cynthia's cheeks reddened, Duffy knew she'd hit a nerve. The doctor *had* warned them all to keep an eye on her.

"I brought you some magazines," Jane said cheerfully, in an effort to ease the awkwardness of the moment. "I hope you haven't read them." She was wearing lime-green pedal pushers and a hot-pink short-sleeved T-shirt with the slogan, GO AHEAD MAKE MY DAY GIVE ME A CHOCOLATE CHIP COOKIE slapped across it in blazing scarlet.

"Don't tell me, let me guess," Duffy said bitterly.

"You brought me the *American Journal of Psychiatric Medicine* and the latest copy of *Guide to Mental Health Facilities*, right?"

A bewildered expression crossed Jane's face. "What? What are you talking about?" She plopped herself down at the foot of Duffy's bed.

"They all think I'm crazy here," Duffy said heatedly. Then she filled Jane in on the shower incident, leaving nothing out, ending with, "It *happened*, Jane. But no one believes me. They all think I was hallucinating."

She didn't add that there were moments when she agreed with them. Right now, talking about it, reliving it, she was convinced that every second of it had been real.

"Oh, Duffy, that's the worst thing I've ever heard!" Jane declared, her eyes wide with horror. "Didn't anyone call the police?" She swallowed a sob. "You could have been *killed!*"

"No one called anyone. I told you, they all think I made it up."

"You wouldn't do that." Staunch loyalty filled Jane's voice. "Why would you lie about something so horrible?"

"No one claims she's lying," Cynthia said. "It's just that everyone on the hospital staff knows what fevers can do, that's all. People see and hear all kinds of weird things when their temperature is sky-high."

Jane looked doubtful. Duffy could see that she didn't know what to believe. How could she blame

Jane for that? She didn't know what to believe herself.

"The shower room door was locked," Cynthia pointed out. "Duffy said so herself. And the extra key was at the nurses' station. So how could anyone have gotten into the room?"

Duffy thought about explaining her key theory and decided against it. Jane looked very upset and confused. What good would it do to keep harping on the same old thing when she couldn't *prove* anything?

"Never mind," she said despondently, "forget I said anything."

Discouraged, depressed, and exhausted from lack of sleep, Duffy was such poor company that Jane and Cynthia stayed only a few minutes. Jane, worry clouding her features, promised to come back later, which gave Duffy an idea, and Cynthia said she would stop in later before she left the hospital.

As they reached the hall, Duffy heard Jane say, "Cyn, Duffy doesn't *invent* things. I can't believe no one is taking her seriously." Then their voices faded and Duffy couldn't hear Cynthia's answer. She was sure it was a calm, sensible one.

But that didn't matter right now. Duffy had thought of a way she could learn something about what was in her capsules.

If Jane was willing to help.

Chapter 15

When Dylan stopped in to see how she was, Duffy fought off her nausea long enough to ask a question that had been tugging at her mind.

"Wouldn't the maintenance crew," she asked as he sat down on her bed, "have a key to the shower room? Besides the ones hanging at the nurses' station, I mean. If a pipe burst or the drain backed up and flooded the place, they'd have to get into that room in a hurry, wouldn't they?"

"Well, if no one was in there, the door wouldn't be locked. They wouldn't need a key to get in."

"Yes, but what if someone was in there when something broke?" she persisted. "And couldn't get to the door to open it. Like . . . like a heart patient who had an attack if . . . if the lights went out. They'd need a key then, wouldn't they?"

"Not really. They'd use the key at the nurses' station. It's hanging in plain sight."

Disappointed with the clear logic of that, Duffy

sighed. "I still think the maintenance crew should have their own key," she grumbled.

Dylan thought for a minute. "They probably did. But stuff gets lost around here every day. I know there's no shower room key hanging in the basement with the other keys."

But maybe there once *had* been. And maybe someone has swiped it. And maybe that someone still *had* that key. . . .

"I'm not so sure you imagined that attack," Dylan said slowly, thoughtfully, surprising her. "I know everyone thinks you were hallucinating, but . . ."

Duffy's eyes filled with tears. It was so wonderful to be believed. She reached out a hand. "You mean it?"

Dylan nodded. "Doesn't seem like you, that's all. I know fevers can do weird things, but it would have to be *some* fever to make Duffy Quinn see things that weren't happening. And I keep thinking, you were able to get up and walk all the way to the shower room, so how bad could your fever have been then? Doesn't seem like it could have been bad enough to make you think someone was trying to kill you."

"Oh, thanks, Dylan," Duffy murmured gratefully. "Thanks! It's so nice to have someone here who doesn't think I've gone off the deep end."

She felt hot again, burning up, ablaze. "Could you hand me a glass of water, please? I'm dying of thirst."

Dylan reached over and lifted the heavy metal carafe, pouring carefully. As he handed her the squat little glass, the sleeve on his green tunic slipped back half an inch, revealing a nasty, jagged scratch on his left wrist.

Duffy's heart stopped. She knew she had made a scratch on her attacker that day in the shower. But Dylan? *Dylan?*

Then she almost laughed aloud. She really *was* losing her mind. Dylan Rourke wouldn't hurt a fly.

Still, after taking a long sip of cool water, she couldn't resist commenting lightly, "That's a wicked cut. What happened?"

Looking annoyed, Dylan shook the sleeve back into its proper place. "Nothing. It's just a scratch."

Unable to stop herself, Duffy pressed on. "From what?" Jokingly, she added, "You weren't trying to end it all, were you, Dylan? I thought I was the loony around here."

His expression of annoyance deepened. "If you must know, it happened when I grabbed your wheelchair. Remember? Just as you were about to go into the lake? Slammed my arm against a rock when the chair dragged me."

Guilt flooded Duffy. He'd hurt himself saving her and here she'd been thinking . . .

Awash in shame, she cried, "Why didn't you *tell* me? No one said you'd been hurt! Honestly," she added in exasperation, "no one tells me anything around here. Did you have a doctor look at that?"

"No. I told you, it's just a scratch. And this is

exactly why I didn't tell you. I knew you'd make a big deal out of it." Then he grinned and took one of her hands in his. "It's nice to know you care about me, though. I wasn't sure. You're not the easiest person to read."

Funny . . . no one else thought that. Everyone else in the hospital seemed to think they knew exactly what was going on in her head and why.

"Of course I care, Dylan," she said and was about to add, "we're friends," when Amy appeared in the doorway.

The expression on her round, pink face told Duffy that Amy had heard her comment about caring for Dylan. She looked stricken. Her eyes were wide and bright with unshed tears, her lower lip quivered, her fists were clenched at her waist.

Duffy thought unhappily, That is not the picture of a girl who cheerfully agreed to end her relationship with Dylan Rourke.

She yanked her hand out of Dylan's grip.

Without a word, Amy turned on her heel and left.

Duffy felt as if she'd just ripped the wings off a butterfly. Amy was clearly still in love with Dylan.

And Dylan was just as clearly interested in Duffy.

"I need to sleep," she told him, her voice curt because of her embarrassment for Amy. "Could you leave?"

It was Dylan's turn to look surprised. "Shouldn't we try to figure out who might have gone after you

in the shower? Maybe someone upstairs got loose."
He gestured to the fifth floor where the psychiatric
ward was. "And if he got loose once, he could again."

"I'm too tired to think about that now, Dylan.
Besides," turning over on her side, "what's the use?
No one will listen, anyway."

He stood up then, laying one hand on the top of
her head. "I think your temperature's up. And
you're right, you need your rest. But I'm going to
think about this, Duffy. If the people in this hospital
aren't safe, someone needs to know that. So stay
right here in this bed, where you'll be safe, okay?
And take your medicine."

She didn't tell him she'd decided not to swallow
one more capsule. He'd argue with her, maybe even
tell one of the doctors or nurses. He might not believe her digoxin theory.

When Dylan had gone, she waited for Jane, who
had promised to return. Hadn't that been hours
ago?

But it was Amy who appeared in the doorway,
carrying Duffy's lunch tray.

They were awkward with each other. Each knew
the other was embarrassed because of the earlier
painful moment, and so both avoided mentioning it.
Their speech was stiff and stilted.

"Here," Amy said, "I brought you a newspaper.
There's an article on the track meet in there. I know
you and Kit always went to all the meets. I thought
you might be interested."

Kit had been a runner in high school, so Duffy

had become interested. And then, after attending several meets, she'd found that she really enjoyed it. After Kit graduated, they sometimes went to meets together.

Kit . . . how she missed him!

"Thanks. Thanks a lot, Amy. I . . ." She would *not* mention Dylan. That would be like twisting a knife in Amy's back. "I think I'll sleep now. I'm really tired."

Unsmiling, Amy moved forward to place the palm of one hand on Duffy's forehead. "You're really hot. Are you taking your pills?"

Duffy knew why everyone was asking her that. The hospital rumor mill had picked up on her suspicions about the capsules. They all figured she'd made up her own mind about the pills and wasn't taking them.

But they couldn't prove it.

"Yes," she said, "I am *taking* my pills." Which wasn't a lie . . . yet.

"See you later," Amy said curtly, obviously not forgiving Duffy for letting Dylan sit on her bed and hold her hand. "Take it easy." She turned on her heel and left, her back as stiff as a board.

And something caught Duffy's eye.

Amy usually wore white stockings to work. She said they made her feel "more professional," more "like a real nurse." But today, she was wearing sheer beige on her legs. And underneath the pale, nearly transparent fabric, Duffy could see, on the back of Amy's leg, an ugly dark red mark, etched across the flesh like a streak of lightning.

"Amy," Duffy called impulsively, "what happened to the back of your leg?"

Amy turned slightly. "What? Oh, that . . . cut myself shaving. Gross, right? Bled all over the place. See you." And she disappeared out the door and into the hall.

I've cut my legs shaving thousands of times, Duffy told herself, but I don't remember ever bleeding "all over the place." And I certainly never made a nasty cut like that. What was Amy shaving with, a power saw?

Or . . . had someone *else* made that cut? Someone desperate, armed with a small pink razor, in the darkness of a puddled shower stall?

What was the matter with her? She really *was* paranoid. If, she thought with disgust, it was my little pink razor that carved that gash in Amy's leg, she wouldn't have been so casual when I asked her about it. And she wouldn't have worn see-through stockings to work today. Or she would have covered the cut with a bandage so I couldn't see it.

Unless . . . unless Amy was so sure of herself, so sure no one believed Duffy's theory about someone being after her, that she felt she had absolutely nothing to hide.

Maybe she even *wanted* Duffy to know it was her. Maybe she was doing a little knife-twisting herself, knowing that a weak, sick person whose sanity was in question would be helpless to stop her.

And Duffy realized with a terrible feeling of

dread that of all the people she knew Amy Severn was the only one with a motive to hurt her. Amy was still in love with Dylan. And Dylan was clearly interested in Duffy.

The police always looked for a motive.

Duffy had just found one.

Chapter 16

Questions about Amy had to be put on hold as Duffy's parents arrived for a quick visit.

"I wish we could come more often," her mother said apologetically. "I worry about you every minute. But it's tax time, honey, and you know what that's like." Duffy's parents were accountants, and she did know what tax time was like. She had picked a lousy time to get sick.

"Can't I please go home?" she begged. "I'll get better faster there, I promise." They hadn't mentioned the shower attack, so she knew the staff had convinced them that it hadn't really taken place. They'd never bring it up, thinking it would upset her further.

"Oh, Duffy, please don't start that again," her mother pleaded. "You're much better off here. I just told you how busy we are. At least here, there's someone watching you every minute."

Well, not really. Where had all the nurses and doctors been the night she'd heard those sounds in her room?

"But I don't feel safe," she protested. "This isn't a safe place to be . . ."

Her parents exchanged worried glances.

She read the gaze. They, too, were concerned that the fever was affecting her mental health.

It was hopeless. She spent the rest of their brief visit in sullen silence and tried not to feel guilty when they left looking uneasy and unhappy. They should have listened to her. . . .

When they had gone, her thoughts returned to Amy. She had thought of Amy as a nice, sweet person, and she *was*, most of the time. But Amy had a temper, Duffy knew that now.

How angry could Amy get?

And had she really cut herself shaving her legs?

Or was she so angry about Dylan's interest in Duffy that she was determined to obliterate the competition?

To escape the questions that had no answers, Duffy picked up the newspaper and began skimming through the track meet article on the sports page. The words had no meaning for her. The fact that Twelvetrees High School's varsity track team would be advancing to the state finals failed to touch her. It seemed unimportant. If Kit were still on the relay team, maybe she'd feel something, in spite of her nerves being strung as tightly as violin strings. But he wasn't.

Where *was* he?

Would he be in California by now? Why hadn't he called to tell her he'd arrived safely and to give her his new address and telephone number? She was glad he'd finally dumped his cranky uncle and whining aunt and that terrible, deadly shoe store. But had he put his best friend, Duffy Quinn, behind along with the rest of Twelvetrees, Maine? Off with the old, on with the new?

No. Kit wouldn't do that.

What would he say to her now, if she told him everything that had happened, and the things she suspected? Would he laugh it off? Tell her, as everyone else had, that she had an overactive imagination or was suffering from fever delirium?

No. He wouldn't do that, either. One of the reasons Kit hadn't been the most popular boy in school was the way he took everything so seriously. Always reading, always learning, taking in new information. He believed that life was not a laughing matter. No wonder, considering the household he lived in.

He would have taken her story seriously. And then he would have tried to help her figure out what to do.

If only she could talk to him now. . . .

Duffy began leafing listlessly through the rest of the newspaper. A name jumped out at her from one of the middle pages, startling her.

Latham. Victor Latham, she read.

Latham? Where had she heard that name before?

The man who had died before she arrived, "Old Man Latham," someone had called him. Her interest piqued, Duffy read the brief article.

A scholarship fund in the name of Victor La-tham, a longtime resident of Twelvetrees and a member of the Community Hospital's Board of Trustees, has been established at the hospital for future medical students. Latham, 64, died recently after a brief illness. According to his daughter and sole survivor, Claire Bristol, Mr. Latham's pri-mary interest in life was medicine. He felt it was important to keep young people interested in ca-reers in the health field. And he was fond of the young people who worked at the hospital while he was ill. The scholarship is being established to re-turn their kindness to him.

Duffy couldn't help wondering which of the "young people" at the hospital had been kind to Victor Latham. Amy? Cynthia? Smith? Maybe even Dylan. Had Latham given any of them money in return for their kindnesses *before* he died? Was that where Smith, an orderly, had found the money to buy that fancy sports car he drove?

Anyway, that night . . . the night she'd heard the clanging of the curtain rings, the *slap-slap* of rubber soles, the clatter of the gurney wheels . . . that hadn't been the night Victor Latham died. So none of the sounds she'd heard had had anything to do with him.

And his death had nothing to do with *her.*

She let the newspaper fall into her blanketed lap.

Victor Latham must have felt very safe here, in the hospital he'd given so much to.

But he *had* died here.

The nurse came in then, armed with the little fluted cup, and briskly handed Duffy the two capsules.

Duffy took them without a word, obediently dipped them into her mouth, tucked them into the flesh of her cheek and prayed silently that the capsules wouldn't dissolve too quickly. She sipped the water handed her by the nurse and slid down beneath the covers, feeling a pressing need for an afternoon nap.

It worked. The nurse turned quietly and left . . . *slap-slap, slap-slap*. The heavy wooden door closed after her.

Duffy sat up and spat the soggy but still intact capsules into the palm of her hand. She wrapped them in a paper napkin and hid the folded napkin under her pillow. She'd have to make sure no one came near it to fluff it or change the pillowcase.

Without the pills, maybe she'd start feeling better.

She was disappointed to find that although dumping the pills gave her some slight feeling of control, she was still unable to relax. Where was Jane, anyway? What was keeping her?

Amy, as bright and cheerful as if the scene between Duffy and Dylan of the day before had never taken place, arrived before Jane. She came breezing into the room, every hair in place, a blue ribbon imprisoning her curls. She was smiling.

Duffy couldn't tell if the smile was real or phony.

"Have you heard?" Amy asked. "Did anyone tell you?"

"Tell me what?"

"Kit called last night. I just heard."

"What? What did you say?"

Amy poured a glass of water for Duffy. "Kit called. To talk to you."

Duffy took the water gratefully. She forgot her suspicions about the cut on Amy's leg. She forgot her hatred for the ugly hospital room and her fear for her own safety. Kit had called?

But before she drank, she said slowly, "But I never talked to Kit last night. The phone didn't ring once. I was awake . . . I would have heard it."

Amy leaned against the nightstand. "They wouldn't put the call through. He forgot the time change between here and California. It was only eight o'clock there, but it was eleven here. The switchboard doesn't put calls through to patients that late at night."

Duffy leaned back against the pillows, weak with disappointment. "Darn! I really wanted to talk to him. He must have read my mind." She smiled slightly. "He could do that, you know. Sometimes. He used to finish my sentences for me. Drove me crazy." She sipped the water slowly, struggling with the bitter news that Kit had actually called, had wanted to talk with her, and hadn't been able to.

"Who took the call?" she asked Amy. Maybe Kit had left a message for her.

Amy shrugged and began straightening the litter

of tissues, hair supplies, get-well cards, and candy boxes that cluttered the nightstand. "Switchboard operator, I guess. One of the nurses told me about it. I thought it would cheer you up, but you don't look very cheerful. Maybe I shouldn't have told you."

"Yes," Duffy said quickly, "yes, you should have. I'm glad you told me." If Kit called again, she didn't want people afraid to tell her. At least now she knew he was okay and had made it to California in one piece. But she was so disappointed at missing his call.

"Thanks, Amy. I hope the operator reminded him of the time change so he won't make the same mistake again."

"I'm sure she did. Maybe he'll call back today." Amy paused and then added, "Dylan knows, Duffy."

Duffy lifted her head. "Knows what?"

"He knows that Kit called here. Everyone knows that some guy from California called you at eleven o'clock last night. I saw Dylan in the hall a few minutes ago and he didn't look happy. He's jealous of Kit, you know. Always has been, even when he was dating . . . me. We argued about it a couple of times."

Before yesterday afternoon, when Amy got so angry with her, Duffy would have had trouble imagining Amy arguing with anyone. But not now.

"I'm sorry," Duffy murmured. "Really, Amy, I am."

"I know." Amy's voice was as soft and sweet as it had always been. "It's okay, Duffy. Not your fault. Look, can I get you anything before I get to work? I might not have time to stop in later. We're pretty busy. More flu cases."

There was something. "Amy, do you remember Victor Latham?"

Amy began fussing with Duffy's blankets. "We're not supposed to talk about him, Duffy. Everyone feels bad that he died. We all liked him. And he was getting better. And then . . ." She shrugged.

"What happened?"

"I don't know. But he was old, and he had a bad heart. So . . ."

Old? The paper had said he was sixty-four. Was sixty-four that old? Duffy's grandmother was seventy-six and still healthy and active.

But then, she didn't have a bad heart.

"Gotta go," Amy said. "Jane'll probably be here in a minute to keep you company. See you later."

She was right. She had barely left the room when Jane hurried in, looking guilty.

"Where have you been?" Duffy cried. "I've been waiting all day for you."

"Sorry." Jane flopped into the bedside chair and put her feet up on the edge of the bed. "Had to run some errands for my father's wife." Jane always used that particular phrase to describe her stepmother, and she rolled her eyes toward heaven as she said the words.

"Well, I'm glad you're in a mood to run errands, because I have one for you," Duffy said. "And it has to be done right this minute."

Jane groaned.

Chapter 17

"Before you tell me what the errand is," Jane said, her lips sliding into a big grin, "I hear you got a telephone call last night. Didn't talking to Kit make you feel better?" Her dark hair was in braids tied with orange ribbon that matched her jumpsuit.

"I never talked to Kit," Duffy explained. "They wouldn't put the call through. Too late. How did you know he called?"

"Dylan told me." A bleak expression flitted across Jane's round, plain face. "He didn't seem too happy about it." She paused and then added, "He likes you, doesn't he?"

Duffy didn't know what to say to that. Yes, he probably *did* like her, but right now, that seemed so unimportant — except to Jane and Amy. Duffy Quinn had far more pressing matters on her mind.

During Jane's absence, Duffy's idea had taken shape. But she needed Jane's help. "Never mind Dylan," she said tersely. "About that errand . . ."

Jane heaved a sigh. "I just got *through* running errands! Is it really, really important?"

"Do you want me to get better?" Duffy asked sternly.

Jane flushed. "Of course I do, Duffy. Okay, what is it? Where do I have to go?"

"To the lab."

Jane frowned. "You mean Dean's lab?"

"Of course. I need a lab, and your brother works in one, so why would I send you to someone else's lab?"

"What do you need a lab for?"

"You're stalling, Jane. Quit asking questions just so you won't have to leave this room. I need my pills analyzed, and Dean's just the person to do it." She handed Jane the capsules she hadn't taken, still wrapped in their paper napkin. "Take these over there, right away, and ask Dean what they are. Then come straight back here and tell me."

Jane's frown deepened. "Why don't you ask your doctor what they are?"

Duffy glared. "Because my doctor doesn't *know* what they are. I mean, he *thinks* he does, but I think he's wrong. I think someone screwed up and gave me the wrong stuff, and Dean can tell me if I'm right. So hurry up, okay? This is important."

Something in her voice sent Jane to her feet. She took the napkin, then hesitated. "Duffy, I can't believe someone would make a mistake like that."

"That's because you aren't a patient in this hospital." Conscious of the minutes passing rapidly, Duffy urged, "Jane, just *do* it, okay? Trust me. I know what I'm doing. I promise, I won't ask you for another single favor as long as I live."

"Yes, you will. And I'll probably give it to you." Jane grinned weakly. "I want you to know I'm only humoring this bizarre request because you're my best friend and I miss you and I want you out of this place so life will be back to normal again. But I'll bet you anything you're wrong about the medication being screwed up, Duffy." She shuddered. "I can't believe someone could make such a mistake."

Duffy shuddered, too. Because she wasn't at all sure it was just a "mistake." She wasn't sure of that at all.

"I'll hurry," Jane said quickly, noticing Duffy's shudder. "I'll tell Dean it's for you. He's always liked you, Duffy." She bent to give Duffy a quick hug. "I'll be right back, I promise."

When Jane had rushed out of the room, Duffy wondered just who she would tell if it turned out that the pills contained the missing digoxin. It would have to be someone she trusted completely. Names flitted through her mind and were rapidly discarded.

The list of people she trusted completely was getting shorter all the time.

A nurse coming in to give Duffy a back rub nearly collided with Jane.

"Where's your friend going in such a big hurry?" she asked amiably as she uncapped the bottle of lotion.

"Gee, I don't know," Duffy fibbed. She wasn't telling a single soul in this place where Jane was going, or why. Not until she was sure of who she could trust.

"You feel hot again," the nurse said as she rubbed Duffy's muscles, so tense with fear and uncertainty, they were cramping between her shoulders. "Your temperature must be up."

Duffy knew it was because she wasn't getting the antibiotics she needed. But until Jane returned with the lab report, she wasn't about to tell anyone she'd quit taking the capsules.

The nurse was leaving when Dylan arrived, mop in hand.

And when he bent to kiss her cheek, Duffy was shocked to find herself recoiling. She didn't do it on purpose. It was strictly an involuntary movement. But she knew it was stimulated by fear.

Fear of *Dylan*?

That really *was* crazy. Dylan hated hurting people. In grade school, he hadn't done well in football because he was so afraid of hurting someone when he tackled them. He'd got over that in high school and was on the varsity team now, but the coach was always yelling at him for "holding back," not "giving his all." Duffy knew it was because he was still a little afraid of breaking bones. Someone *else's* bones, not his own.

It would take something really powerful to overcome Dylan's reluctance to hurt people.

And she couldn't think of a single thing powerful enough to do that.

But neither could she bring herself to return his

kiss, or even smile as if she meant it, not until she felt completely safe — if she ever did again.

How long would Jane's "errand" take?

Frowning, Dylan asked gently, "You okay? Taking your pills?"

Wearing a frown of her own, Duffy remembered that this wasn't the first time Dylan had asked that question. Why was he so preoccupied with her medication?

Maybe, she thought, her stomach twisting in revulsion, maybe he knew something about those pills. . . .

"Yes," she snapped, "I'm taking them."

Could Dylan, who seemed to like her so much, be the one who wanted to hurt her? What reason would he have?

If Kit were still around, maybe jealousy would make Dylan act weird, do strange things.

But Kit was in California. He wasn't a threat to Dylan. Not that he ever had been, but Dylan didn't know that. Maybe he was the sort of person who didn't believe girls could have male *friends*. Like Jane, who had always had a hard time believing that Duffy and Kit weren't in love.

"If you don't want him for a boyfriend," she had said more than once, "you shouldn't monopolize his time when there are so many girls out there without boyfriends."

Meaning Jane, of course.

But Kit had never been attracted to Jane. Duffy had suggested once, casually, that Kit ask her out, and he had said, "I don't think so. She's not my type."

Meaning he liked "thinkers" and Jane wasn't a thinker. She was a "feeler," running mostly on emotion. Kit, who lived in a household devoid of emotion, couldn't understand that.

Dylan wasn't happy when he left her room, but Duffy couldn't dwell on that.

Where was Jane? I need to know the truth, Duffy thought, and I need to know it *now.*

A very long hour and a half later, she did. Because Jane, red-cheeked and breathless, came into the room carrying a brown paper bag.

"Well, here it is," she said wearily. She handed the bag to Duffy. "The pills are in there, and so is the report. Dean was glad to do it . . . for you." She hesitated, and then added in a voice that hinted of hurt feelings, "Duffy, why didn't you tell me you had a heart condition?"

Duffy looked down at the slip of paper in her hand, already knowing what it said.

DIGOXIN

Chapter 18

Duffy tried to still her racing heart. She told herself it wasn't as if she hadn't suspected . . . the word DIGOXIN shouldn't have been that great a shock.

But it was.

Seeing it there on the small slip of paper, seeing the proof that her suspicions, which had once seemed so wild, had been accurate after all, punched her in the stomach. Someone had actually done this to her? On purpose? Sent this awful, sickening drug flowing through her body?

Who could hate her that much?

She had been right. Someone had switched the digoxin with her antibiotics. Someone had actually stolen her pills, split the capsules in two, emptied out the "something-myocin," and replaced the antibiotic with the missing digoxin.

And no one knew that but her.

Except for the person who had *done* it.

Who *was* that person?

As she stared, frozen, at the slip of paper in her hand, Jane repeated her question. "Duffy? Why didn't you tell me you had a heart condition?"

"I don't," Duffy replied. "There's nothing wrong with my heart." Except that it was pounding wildly in her chest.

"Dean made a mistake? But . . . but he seemed so sure," Jane said. "I mean, I told him digoxin didn't sound like an antibiotic, and he said it wasn't. He said it was heart medication. I said you didn't have anything wrong with your heart, and he said, 'Then she shouldn't be taking this stuff. It won't make her well. It'll make her *sicker*.' "

Duffy said nothing. She was debating whether or not to take Jane into her confidence. What if, in spite of Dean's analysis, Jane didn't believe her. What if she wrote it off as a simple mistake and accused Duffy of "paranoia"? Worse, what if she *told* someone that Duffy had had the pills tested? Word would spread quickly through the hospital that Duffy knew the truth . . . once whoever had done this knew Duffy was on to them, something really terrible might happen. Maybe to *Jane*, because she had taken the pills to the lab.

No. She couldn't tell Jane. It was too risky.

"Never mind," Duffy said, "let's forget it. Let's talk about something else. Seen Dylan today?"

"Duffy!" Jane squealed. "Are you kidding? Dean tells me you're taking heart medication, and you say you don't have a heart condition, and you expect me to forget it, just like that? What's going on?"

When Duffy, her mind racing to come up with a plausible explanation that would keep Jane safe, failed to respond, Jane pressed. "Duffy, we don't keep secrets from each other, right? Are you in some kind of trouble? You sounded so scared earlier. What are you doing with those pills? Where did you get them?"

Duffy wanted desperately to confide in Jane. She was so tired of worrying alone. And what was the point of having a best friend if you couldn't tell her the truth?

But what kind of friend were you if you deliberately put your best friend in danger?

A rotten kind of friend.

She couldn't stand the thought of anything terrible happening to Jane. Bad enough that Kit had left. What would she do without Jane?

Forcing a grin onto her face, she said, "Gotcha!" and added slyly, "Does the phrase 'wild-goose chase' have any meaning for you?"

It took Jane a few minutes. When the words finally sank in, her cry of outrage echoed throughout the room. "Dorothy Leigh Quinn! I don't *believe* this! You didn't! You didn't send me all the way across town for no reason, did you?"

Duffy's grin splashed wider.

Jane flopped back in her chair, throwing her hands up in the air. "This is not happening. Sick people are not supposed to play stupid practical jokes. I do *not* believe this."

But Duffy could see that she did. And her relief was mixed with a terrible sense of loneliness. She had kept Jane out of it. Jane was safe. But now she was alone again, with no one on her side.

"Honestly, Duffy," Jane babbled, "this is just like

the time you told me Michael J. Fox was making a personal appearance here and if I hurried, I could get tickets." The corners of her lips began to turn up in the birthing of a laugh. Glaring at Duffy in mock anger, she said, "You laughed *so* hard. I thought you'd crack a rib."

Then she added with a grin, "So, I guess this means you're getting better, right? And you'll be sprung soon?" Her voice softened, "I miss you something fierce, Duff. I hate it when you pull this kind of stunt, but nothing's the same when you're not around."

Thinking of the digoxin in her system, Duffy fell silent. *Would* she be going home soon? Would she be going home at *all*? In one piece?

She needed to think about what the lab report meant, and what to do about it. "I'm really all worn out," she told Jane. "I think I need to sleep for a while. Maybe you could come back tonight?"

Immediately, Jane jumped to her feet. "Oh, sure. I'm sorry. I shouldn't have stayed so long. I keep forgetting you're sick. I'll come back later." Her smile then was sweet to see. "I'm mad at you for sending me across town for nothing, but I'm glad that you felt well enough to do it. 'Bye."

Duffy watched her go, her thick dark hair swinging on her shoulders, and was glad she'd made up that silly story about a wild-goose chase. Being in this alone wasn't easy, but at least she didn't have to worry about something horrible happening to Jane.

Alone again, she asked herself if the digoxin in

her pills could possibly have been a mistake.

There had been a lot of "mistakes" — the elevator sign being switched, the wheelchair being pushed down the hill, the attack in the shower, the digoxin. There was no way all of those things could be simple mistakes. Someone had engineered them.

If only she had some clue as to who it was, and why.

Duffy settled back against the pillow, her head throbbing, and closed her eyes.

As hard as it was to believe, Duffy realized with horror, it had to be someone she knew, someone who'd been around the hospital and knew where she was and what she was doing.

Amy was still in love with Dylan, that was obvious. But Dylan was interested in the ailing Duffy Quinn. That must either hurt Amy terribly . . . or make her very angry. And she had a temper, Duffy knew that now. She also had a very nasty scratch on the back of her leg.

How far would Amy Severn go to get Dylan Rourke back?

Dylan had a cut, too. On his wrist. He had said he'd hurt himself when he saved her from hurtling into the chilly waters of the lake.

But Dylan had no reason to hurt her, did he? What had she ever done to Dylan?

Amy had said Dylan was jealous of her friendship with Kit, had been for a long time. *How* jealous? And why would that make Dylan want to hurt *her*?

Could Dylan and Kit have had an argument before Kit left? Was Dylan hiding a hatred of Kit so deep that he would attack anyone who was close to Kit? Duffy Quinn, for instance?

But . . . wouldn't that mean Dylan was severely unhinged? If he was, he hid it well.

If she only had Kit's phone number, she could call him and find out if Dylan and he had fought.

What about Cynthia? She seemed to be interested only in Duffy's health. But was that just a clever disguise? Duffy tried to recall something she might have done to anger Cynthia. But she came up with nothing.

There was Smith Lewis, too. He had been there at the empty elevator shaft, and again behind her wheelchair on the hill. As far as she knew, Smith had no reason to want her out of the way. And he had seemed so helpful. . . .

What am I *doing*? Duffy covered her face with her hands. Everyone is right about me, she thought in disgust. I *am* losing it. Suspecting my friends, people who have helped me since I got sick. No wonder everyone is treating me as if I've gone off the deep end. Ever since that night I heard those weird noises in my room.

Those noises . . . that night . . . the sounds . . . what if everyone was wrong and those sounds hadn't been figments of her fevered mind's imagination? What if there really *was* someone in her room? Someone who didn't want to be seen? Someone who was afraid Duffy *had* seen him? Or her?

But . . . what could that someone have been doing in her room that was so awful, killing the only witness had become absolutely necessary?

"Fooling around" with a date, as Jane had suggested, couldn't be it. That was ridiculous. Whatever had happened in her room, if anything had, it had been a lot deadlier than a few stolen kisses.

What *was* it?

Had she really seen something? And forgotten it because it was too awful to remember?

And who, exactly, had she shared the experience with? Who knew she'd heard something that night?

Everyone.

Everyone knew.

Duffy felt tears of exasperation stinging her eyelids. What difference did it make? Why waste time racking her brain to figure out who wanted her sick or dead, when it was so clear that the only way to be safe was to escape from the hospital.

Now that she knew the digoxin in her body had been put there deliberately, she couldn't spend one more night in this place.

She had to get away.

I am not, she thought with resolve, spending another night lying awake, waiting. If only I could call Kit, tell him to come and get me. He would. And he wouldn't ask any questions until we were safely out of here.

But Kit wasn't here.

She would have to figure out, all by herself, how to carry out her resolution to leave this place.

Chapter 19

Duffy decided on the midnight hour to attempt her escape. The patients would be asleep by then, the nurses occupied with night care and writing reports. She would have to be careful to steer clear of the maintenance crew. On her sleepless nights, she'd heard them out in the halls at all hours, mopping the floors or changing light fixtures. Any one of them would be suspicious of a patient lurking in the corridor at such a late hour. They might report her, clip her wings before she took flight.

That couldn't happen. She *had* to get out of here.

Her skin, hot and dry to the touch, felt too tight. It squeezed against her, a bodysuit one size too small. The hands on her watch crawled slowly, slowly, as if struggling through glue. Seven o'clock, eight . . .

When her parents came, she asked once more if they would take her home. She knew they wouldn't. They trusted the hospital completely, or they wouldn't have brought her here in the first place.

"If you would just relax, Duffy," her mother scolded lightly, "you'd get better so much faster. Dr. Morgan says it's nothing serious, but that you're impeding your own recovery."

Impeding her own recovery? *She* wasn't the one doing the impeding!

Knowing she would just upset her parents if she kept insisting that she wasn't safe in the hospital, Duffy gave up. She'd get out of this place on her own if it was the last thing she ever did.

Jane never arrived. When Cynthia came in later that evening to bring Duffy fresh water, she said Jane had called the nurses' station to say she wasn't feeling well.

"Didn't you get her message?" Cynthia asked when Duffy's face registered distress. Jane, ill? Duffy thought. She'd been perfectly fine that afternoon.

"People around here don't seem to be very good about delivering messages," Duffy said dourly. "I almost never found out that Kit had called, either. Did Jane say what's wrong with her? I hope I didn't give her my bug."

Cynthia shook her head. "Maybe she was just tired. All that running around she did for you today. I saw her come in and go back out and then come in again. Did she bring you goodies?"

Hardly, Duffy thought. She brought me the news that someone is out to get me. Aloud, she said, "No. Just shampoo."

Cynthia nodded, said she was going home soon

and she'd see Duffy in the morning, and then she left.

You won't see *me* in the morning, Duffy thought to herself, because I'll be long gone. I *hope*.

When the last visitor had left, the eerie silence she was waiting for crept, foglike, across the fourth floor until the last soft murmur had been swallowed up. Duffy tiptoed to her closet and slipped inside, dressing in the dark, narrow space: jeans, a sweater, socks, sneakers. Leaving her gown on the floor of the closet, she hurried back to the bed and slid under the covers to wait for the perfect moment.

She had no plan. There was no way to plan without knowing exactly where everyone might be at every second. She would wait and be very careful and do a lot of praying and hoping. If she could make it to the elevator without being seen. . . .

"You still awake?" a voice said from the doorway.

Duffy jumped, startled, and quickly yanked the blanket up to hide the telltale sweater. "Smith? What are you doing here?"

He came into the room, moving toward the bed. In the weak glow of the night-light beside the door, she could see his grin. "Checking up on you," he answered. Noticing the blanket tucked up underneath her chin, he frowned. "You cold? Doesn't seem that bad in here to me."

"*You* don't have a fever," she pointed out. "One minute I'm burning up, the next I'm freezing. Right now, I'm freezing." She could hear the tension in her voice. Would Smith pick up on it? What if he got suspicious?

She had left the closet door open. Jerk! If he glanced in and noticed that her clothes weren't hanging on the hangers . . .

He wasn't looking at the closet. He was looking down at her.

What if he decided to check her pulse? He did that sometimes — showing off, playing "doctor." If he did that now, he'd be surprised to find her wrist encased in a sweater cuff.

She'd just have to say she'd been so cold, she'd thrown a sweater on over her hospital gown.

"How come you're not asleep?" he asked.

"It's hard to sleep when someone's standing over your bed talking to you," Duffy said sarcastically. And was surprised to see Smith recoil, as if she'd struck him. Had she hurt his feelings? Did it matter?

Maybe some other time it would. But not now, not when her life was on the line. The only thing that mattered was getting away from here, and she couldn't do that with Smith Lewis standing over her bed. If it took hurting his feelings to get rid of him, so be it.

"Sorry," he said stiffly. "Didn't mean to bother you. Thought you might need something." He hesitated and then added, "I . . . I wanted to make sure you knew I did check the brake on your wheelchair. I've thought about it, and I'm sure of it."

The horror of that terrifying ride swept back over Duffy, and she shuddered violently.

"Sorry," Smith said for a second time. "Shouldn't have brought it up. Probably still gives you nightmares. No wonder you can't sleep."

Even in the darkened room, she could see the guilt in his face. But how could she be sure he was sincere? Of course he would say he'd checked the brake. He certainly wouldn't admit it if he'd deliberately sent that chair racing down the hill.

"I *could* sleep," she said caustically, "if you'd go away and leave me alone."

"Your tough act doesn't fool me," Smith said quietly. "I think you're scared to death, and I don't blame you. You've had a rough time. Fevers can be nasty things."

Fever? Duffy thought nastily. It wasn't my fever that switched the signs on the elevator or sent me down that hill or came after me in the shower. Who is he kidding?

"Say you believe I checked that brake and I'll get out of here," he said, bending low over the bed. "I need to know you believe it."

"Sure. I believe you." Anything to get rid of him. "In fact, I'm pretty sure I *saw* you check the brake." Actually, she thought now that she *had* seen him check it. But maybe what she'd really seen was Smith sabotaging the brake so that it would release and send her flying down the hill toward the lake shortly after he was safely away from the scene.

But she must have sounded convincing because Smith heaved a sigh of relief. "Great! Okay, then. You sleep now and I'll check on you when I come on duty tomorrow." Then he caught her by surprise by bending quickly and kissing her cheek.

Before she could protest, he was gone. She could hear the soft *slap-slap* of his rubber-soled shoes as he disappeared down the dim hallway.

Duffy found herself wishing fervently that she could somehow be sure that Smith was on her side. Then she could ask him to help her make her mad dash for freedom and she wouldn't be so terrified. But . . .

Smith had been the only person near the elevator, and he'd been the only person close to her wheelchair. How could she possibly trust him?

No, better to do it alone. She'd be safer that way.

But she didn't *feel* safe when, some twenty minutes later, she listened and listened again and then slid out of bed, put on her ski jacket, and tiptoed to the doorway to listen once more.

Nothing. Silence. Not a total silence . . . she could faintly hear the sound of murmuring voices. Nurses, probably. But they sounded too far away to be at the nurses' station, where they could see her as she passed. Maybe they were in some patient's room, and if the door was nearly closed, as hers always was at night, she should be able to slip by unnoticed.

If she could just make it to the elevator. . . .

Duffy's skin pinched at her again. What if someone were in the elevator? Maybe she should try for the stairs. They were hidden behind a steel door in the middle of the corridor, closer to her room than the elevator at the end of the hall.

But they'd be dark. Wouldn't they? And she had no flashlight.

The elevator was faster.

Faster seemed better.

Her heart went on a rampage in her chest, thudding so violently she wouldn't have been surprised to see it leap out and land on the floor at her feet. Her hands, icy cold in spite of the fever that raged in her body, shook as she pressed her back so close to the wall she seemed almost a part of it, and began moving slowly, slowly, down the hall.

Her teeth began to chatter, and she bit her tongue. She felt warm blood on her lower lip. Another step, another . . .

"You take this side, I'll take the other," a voice Duffy recognized said. The ponytailed nurse. The remark came from inside one of the rooms.

Duffy inched her way right up to the door of the room from which the voices came. The door was half open. If they saw her passing . . .

Slowly, carefully, she peered around the corner of the door frame. Two nurses . . . their backs turned to the door . . .

Holding her breath, Duffy skittered past the door and stopped on the opposite side, paralyzed.

She waited for one of them to call out, "Hey, there, you! Duffy Quinn! What are you doing skulking around in the halls? Get back to your room this minute."

But no one called out.

They hadn't seen her.

Breathing again, the violent trembling slightly eased, she continued her turtle-pace down the hallway. After what seemed like agonizing hours, she was within two steps of the elevator.

Just two more steps . . .

"Going somewhere?" a voice said in her ear.

Chapter 20

Duffy froze in place. Nononono! Not when she was this *close* . . . one more step and she'd have reached the elevator button.

But now . . .

Reluctantly, awash in bitter disappointment, she turned to face the person who had interrupted her flight.

Dylan.

Dylan frowned at her, his square, open face full of concern. "Duffy, I can tell by your eyes that your fever isn't down. What are you doing out of bed?" He had changed from the green smock into street clothes, a sweater and jeans. Going off duty, like Smith. Could she talk Dylan into taking her with him?

Duffy, her energy sapped by the fever and her disappointment, sagged against the wall.

Dylan reached out and held her around the waist. "Whoa, easy there! How come you're dressed? Why aren't you asleep?" Then, "Boy, you're burning up!

Geez, Duffy, are you nuts or what? You should be in bed."

She had to trust him. She had no choice. If she didn't tell him what was happening, if she couldn't convince him that someone was after her, he'd lead her back to her room and she'd belong to the hospital again. And she wouldn't be safe.

Dylan wouldn't hurt her. They'd been friends for a long time. How could she have suspected him? He had the nicest face in the world, and he had covered up the truth about his breakup with Amy to protect her feelings. That had been a kind thing to do. Someone like that would certainly help her, wouldn't he?

So she poured it all out. "Dylan, listen," she began, clinging desperately to his arm, "I can't stay here. I have to go home. Please, you have to help me. You can take me there. Then I can tell them about the lab report . . ."

"What lab report?"

"Jane took my pills to a lab today, and I was right . . . they had digoxin in them . . . the missing heart medication. You heard about it, didn't you? That it was missing?"

Dylan nodded.

"Well, someone took it and put it in my capsules. I said I was getting sicker, but no one believed me. So I asked Jane to get them tested, and she did. And the lab report said just what I knew it would . . . that there wasn't any antibiotic in the capsules I was taking. Just digoxin. That's what was making me sicker."

"Duffy . . ." Dylan's voice registered doubt, but

he kept his arm around her waist. She couldn't have remained standing without it.

"No, listen, *please*! Someone here, I don't know why, is trying to kill me. I didn't imagine the attack in the shower, Dylan, the way everyone thinks I did. It really happened." Tears of frustration gathered in Duffy's eyes and spilled down her fever-pinked cheeks. "*All* of it really happened. Someone switched the out-of-order sign on purpose and someone pushed my chair down the hill on purpose — "

"Duffy, take it easy." Dylan's voice was gentle and quiet as he gathered her closer against his chest.

"You have to believe me, Dylan. You're the only one I can trust."

Dylan flushed with pleasure. "How about if you show me that lab report? It's not that I don't believe you, Duffy, but seeing that would help. I mean, it's hard to believe that someone would give you the wrong medication."

"Of course, you're right. Here . . ." Duffy gasped as she slid a hand into her jeans pocket. It was empty. "The report . . . I must have left it on the bed. Dylan, I have to have it. It's the proof that my capsules were switched."

A nurse came out of a patient's room and hurried to the nurses' station. But Duffy and Dylan were standing in shadow and weren't seen.

"We'll just go get the report," Dylan whispered. "Then you'll have it to show your folks. I'll take you home, if you're sure that's what you want to do."

"I'm sure, Dylan, oh, I'm sure! But . . . I don't

think I can make it back down the hallway again. I'm too tired. Could you just go get the report . . . it's on my bed, probably hiding in the covers? I'll wait here. I'll hide over there in that corner until you get back. Hurry, okay? I feel like I'm going to pass out any minute."

The last bit of doubt faded from Dylan's blue eyes. "Okay. Stay right here, don't move. I'll be right back."

And he hurried off down the hallway as Duffy moved to take refuge behind a tall white column disguising a heating duct.

It was almost over. Dylan would come back with the report, take her home, and her parents would take it from there.

Relief washed over her, and her hands finally stopped shaking. It was going to be all right. It was. Whoever was doing this to her would be caught, and put away somewhere where they couldn't do bad things anymore.

And she'd find out why all of this had happened. But best of all, she'd be safe, the way she used to be. Duffy closed her eyes.

Suddenly, Duffy heard voices approach.

"I'll take care of her," a crisp, efficient voice said.

And Duffy looked into the face of the middle-aged head nurse. In her right hand was a hypodermic needle. "You go on home, Rourke. You did the right thing. This poor child shouldn't even be out of bed. She'll be fine now, thanks to you."

Duffy drew in her breath and took a step backward. "No, no," she murmured, her horrified eyes flying to stare accusingly at Dylan, who lingered behind the nurse. "You — you promised!"

"There wasn't any report," he said, his eyes pleading for forgiveness. "Honest, Duffy, I looked and looked. There wasn't anything! You must have thought there was, but there wasn't."

Duffy continued to back away until she ran into the wall. The nurse continued to advance, needle in hand.

"Call Jane!" Duffy begged, her eyes wildly searching for a way out. There was none. "Call Jane, she'll tell you! She'll tell you she had the pills analyzed and that Dean said they had heart medication in them." Her voice rose to a piercing scream. "Dylan, *call* her!"

"He's not calling anyone at this hour, Dorothy," the nurse said briskly, "and you just calm down now. This isn't doing you any good at all. You quiet down and let us take care of you. You should thank your friend here instead of shouting at him like that. He probably saved your life. Going out on a cold night like this with that fever of yours . . . why, heavens, child, that's just crazy!"

And in the next instant, with Duffy safely trapped between the wall and the nurse's bulk, her sleeve was pushed up and in went the needle. Duffy, devastated by Dylan's treachery, felt the sharp, piercing sensation and began sobbing, "No, no, oh no. . . ."

The nurse, saying, "There, there, now, there's no need for this, no need at all," took one arm, and Dylan, worry in his eyes, took the other, and they began leading Duffy down the hall toward her room.

"Duffy," Dylan said, "don't be mad, okay? When I couldn't find the report, I figured you'd been, well, thinking things had happened again that really hadn't. I mean, like you did before, remember? Remember, there really wasn't anyone in your room that night, but you thought there was?"

"I hate you, Dylan!" Duffy spat. "I hate you for this! I trusted you . . ."

But then the medication from the needle began to kick in, and the lights in the hallway began to spin, and the walls began weaving, and Duffy's legs gave way. By the time they reached her room, her captors were half carrying, half dragging her.

"Dylan," she murmured as they carefully deposited her boneless, drugged body on the bed, "I won't ever . . ." What was it she wanted to say? It was so hard to think, with her brain all fuzzy and sticky. "Dylan, I won't ever forgive you. Never, never . . ."

And, as her voice faded out and a thick, gluey sleep took over, she knew that she meant it.

Even if he hadn't done the other bad things, even if he had meant to do the right thing, even if he told her a million times how sorry he was . . .

She would never forgive Dylan.

More asleep than awake, Duffy floated on a thick, dark gray cloud. Fighting to resist the drug, unwilling to give up hope, she lay on her back in the darkened room, her head filled with fog, her arms and legs heavy as cement.

Slap-slap, slap-slap . . . footsteps whispered toward her bed.

"What . . . ?" Duffy murmured woozily, "what?" Was it Dylan, returning to apologize?

There was a slight rustling noise. The mattress sagged beneath Duffy as an added weight clambered aboard and settled itself across Duffy's stomach.

"What? What's happening . . ."

There was no time to scream, no chance to fight. Without warning, her pillow was yanked out from underneath her head. Duffy grunted in surprise as her head fell backward, flat upon the mattress.

Then something soft and thick and suffocating was pressed down upon her nose and mouth and held there with great force, completely cutting off her air supply.

Duffy Quinn couldn't breathe.

Chapter 21

As the pillow pressed down cruelly over Duffy's nose and mouth, she began flailing about wildly with her arms, the only limbs not pinioned by the weight on her legs and stomach. But her hands, searching the air desperately for help, grasped only empty, useless space.

Frantic, she sent her hands to the pillow covering her face. She clawed at the worn fabric . . . pulled . . . tugged . . . while her entire body bucked and heaved in an effort to dislodge the weight pinning her down.

But it was no use. Weakened from her illness, her reflexes slowed by the sedative, Duffy had no more strength than a small child.

Guttural sounds of panic stuck in her throat, held prisoner there by the pillow viciously shoving her lips back against her teeth. Her upper lip felt as if it were being cut to ribbons.

Air . . . air . . . there was no air . . .

No no no no . . . this couldn't happen . . . she

couldn't die now . . . not now . . . not yet . . .

Her hands abandoned their futile tug-of-war with the pillow and again searched the air for aid.

Her right hand slammed into the bedside table. The table . . . the hand rose tentatively to the table surface, the fingers scrambled across the Formica, feeling, searching . . .

Something cold and hard . . . the carafe, the heavy metal jug that held her water.

Red and purple spots danced before her eyes, the lids pressed harshly into the sockets. The pain in her chest was unbearable. Her lungs were going to explode . . .

Her fingers closed around the handle of the metal carafe, gripped it tightly.

But her arm . . . her arm had no strength. Weak and drugged, her muscles refused what her brain in desperation, willed them to do.

The spots increased, a cloud of red and purple and now yellow, bright yellow . . . she was going to pass out.

Move, she screamed to the arm holding the carafe, move, dammit!

Her arm moved. It moved across the space from the table to the bed, it moved up, up, up and, as Duffy felt herself beginning to fade away into the cloud of red and purple and yellow, the arm slammed the carafe blindly downward.

There was a sickening thud as the carafe smacked into a skull. A surprised grunt of pain echoed in the room, and the weight on Duffy's legs and stomach shifted slightly as her captor swayed, stunned, above her. The suffocating grip on the pillow eased.

Duffy gulped for air. She knew she had only seconds — her attacker hadn't been knocked unconscious. In another second or two, the smothering attack would be renewed with angry vigor. The time to move was *now*.

Duffy shoved upward on the pillow, knocking it away from her. She could see nothing but the dim shadow of a figure sitting, tilted sideways, above her.

Still gasping, her chest heaving in pain, Duffy brought her drug-heavy legs upward, her knees lifting her attacker further off balance. The precariously tilted figure uttered an oath and went flying up and sideways, off the bed in an arc. It landed on the tile floor with a muttered "Oosh!" There was a sharp crack, and the room fell silent.

Free at last, Duffy threw herself out of the bed, landing on the floor in a heap. Lurching, she scrambled upward, clutching the bed for support. Then she staggered to the doorway.

A moan from behind her sent her reeling outward, into the dimly lit hall. Clutching the wall for support, her drug-dulled eyes searched the corridor for signs of life.

Nothing. Quiet as a . . . tomb. . . .

Dizzy and dazed, Duffy stumbled down the hall, the wall her only source of support. She tried to hurry. That moan had meant her attacker was regaining consciousness. Any second now, someone would be pursuing her, and she was moving so slowly . . . so slowly . . .

If she could just make it to the stairs, open the heavy door, close it behind her before anyone saw her . . .

There would be no support as she crossed from the wall to the door. What if she fell? A fall now would destroy any chance of escape.

I *won't* fall, she told herself, biting her already sore lower lip.

She didn't fall. But for one awful, terrible minute when she reached the door, she thought she wasn't going to be able to open it. It was so heavy. And she was so very, very tired. Her arms and legs seemed to weigh a ton.

Somehow, she managed to pull the door open and stumble into the landing, watching in terror as the door took forever to close, so slowly, after her. When it had, she clung to the iron railing and allowed herself a tiny sigh of relief. She was hidden from view now. If her attacker had revived enough to venture out into the hallway, there would be no sign of Duffy.

Now . . . to get down the stairs and find a door leading to the outside . . . and freedom.

She was on the fourth floor . . . one, two, three flights of gray stone steps to the first floor.

No . . . she shouldn't leave the stairway at the first floor. That was the lobby. There would be a security guard at the door, another person who wouldn't believe her and would send her back to her room — and into the hands of her attacker.

Better to continue down one more flight and sneak out through the basement. There had to be a door down there somewhere. She would find one.

If she could get that far without falling on her face . . .

Hurry! She'd forgotten, for a moment, the need to hurry.

Down the steps . . . not enough light . . . only a small yellow light at the top of the landing . . . maybe on each of the landings . . . she needed more light, but at least it wasn't pitch-black.

Hard to see each step . . . dizzy, so dizzy, so headachey, chest hurts, but . . . hurry, hurry . . .

She was stumbling around the corner of the second landing when she heard the unmistakable sound of the heavy steel door above her opening.

Duffy froze.

Light from the hallway on the fourth floor bathed the staircase in a pale yellow glow as the door was held open.

Duffy shrank back against the wall in an effort to hide.

The pale glow disappeared slowly as the door swung shut.

And the sound of soft footsteps moving quickly downward echoed in the silence of the stairway.

Her pursuer had arrived.

Duffy, her heart pounding dangerously, swallowed a sob of terror and lurched away from the wall and down the stairs, her legs heavy and unsteady. She slammed against the steel railing more than once, banging an elbow or a wrist, but she kept going, her breath coming unevenly in harsh gasps.

And behind her the soft, threatening steps continued.

Chapter 22

Duffy stepped too hard as she reached the last step leading to the basement, jarring her body and nearly falling to her knees. Regaining her balance, she spied a door at the end of a long, narrow corridor of smooth cement walls. One small fluorescent ceiling fixture did a poor job of illuminating the entire length, and the space was unheated. It was very cold.

The door beckoned to her. Although Duffy shivered from the chill as she moved in a jerky run, the damp, cold air helped pull her further from her drugged fog. She was going to make it. She *was*.

The *slap-slap* on the stairs behind her moved closer. And there was a new sound now . . . a cheerful humming . . . her pursuer was humming!

What kind of person hummed on his way to kill someone?

Was he that sure that he would catch her?

That made her angry and fired her movements, speeding them up slightly.

The door had to be open. It *had* to!

It was. She reached it just as the padded footsteps behind her left the stairs and hit the cement floor. The difference in the sound was unmistakable. That put him at one end of the corridor, which he could cross far more quickly than she had, and her at the opposite end.

But the door was hers now. In one more second, she'd be outside.

Would her pursuer follow her outside?

Would he feel, as she did, that if she made it to the outside, she'd won? Would he then give up?

Or would he find some way to kill her out there, too?

The humming behind her increased in volume, the footsteps *slap-slapped* closer. "Dorothy," a voice whispered, "give up. You can't get away from me. Give up now."

Give up? Never!

She closed her hand around the doorknob and yanked, hard. It opened easily.

But . . . not to the outside.

Bitter disappointment washed over her as she yanked the door closed behind her and stared at a cold white room: white tiled floor, white walls, white ceiling. There was only one light, high on the far wall, casting yellowish shadows over all that white. The space in the center of the wide, square room was taken up with three tables on wheels. The wall nearest Duffy was filled, ceiling to floor, with small metal doors with latches.

And then Duffy, with a sharp gasp of horror, realized where she was.

She was in the morgue.

She was in the room where they brought the patients who had died. There, Dylan had told her, the patients were kept, until other arrangements could be made, on tables that slid in and out of the small steel cabinets.

"Oh, no," she sobbed softly, her hands covering her face, "oh, God, I don't want to be here!"

But when she turned to retreat, the doorknob was already turning. A second later, the door swung open.

Cynthia Boon stood on the threshold.

Still in her blue uniform, her hair neatly fastened behind her ears, her thin face pale and tired-looking, she stared at Duffy with concern in her eyes. Her arms embraced a thick pile of grayish-white towels.

"Duffy, what on earth are you doing down here?" she cried.

Weak with relief, Duffy sagged against the wall. "I have never been so glad to see anyone in my *life*!" she said. Then, glancing nervously around Cynthia toward the door, she whispered, "Didn't you run into anyone out there?"

Cynthia looked at the door. "Out where?"

"Out in the *hall*. Wasn't there anyone out there?"

"Duffy, it's almost one o'clock in the morning. No one in his right mind would be wandering the basement halls. What are you doing down here?"

She can take me home, Duffy thought, her brain working more quickly as the drug wore off. She can drive me to my house where I'll be safe.

"Take me home and I'll tell you. I know it will

sound crazy, but every word is the truth and you have to believe me." Duffy's words rushed together in her effort to convince Cynthia to drive her home. "Just take me home, please, Cynthia. . . ."

Cynthia raised her hands in a gesture of defeat. "Okay, I give up. The whole hospital gives up! We're all tired of trying to make you well when you have all these crazy notions in your head that someone is out to get you. You might just as well go home. I'm through here for the night, so I'll — " She stopped. "Duffy? What's the matter?"

Duffy, frozen in place against the square metal doors, was staring, white-faced, at Cynthia's left wrist.

Just above where the sleeve of her blue blouse ended, there was a two-inch ugly, jagged cut, fresh enough not to be healed.

"Cynthia?" Duffy asked through numbed lips. "Where did you get that cut?"

And Cynthia sighed and smiled, a smile that never went near her suddenly cold, empty eyes.

"I got it in the shower," she said lightly. Her smile widened. "I don't know why they call them safety razors, Duffy, do you? There certainly wasn't anything safe about *that* razor."

And she began moving slowly toward Duffy, a look of cold purpose on her pale, thin face.

Chapter 23

"You?" Duffy croaked, shrinking back against the wall of metal drawers. "You were the one who . . . in the shower . . . no . . ." She shook her head. Her cinnamon-colored hair seemed to stand on end. "No . . . we're friends, Cynthia. I've never done anything to you. Why . . . ?"

"Because of Kit, of course." Cynthia slipped one hand into a pocket of her blue uniform.

"Kit?" Duffy's fever-flushed face registered complete bewilderment. "What about Kit?"

Cynthia's hand moved within the pocket, as if she were fingering something. "You're the only one who knows what really happened to him." She shrugged. "You can't really figure it out right now, of course. But you will. Probably when your fever goes down for good, you'll figure out what you heard and saw in your room that night." Another shrug. "I can't take that chance."

Duffy licked her lips nervously. "Cynthia, I don't know what you're talking about. Nothing happened to Kit. He's fine. He called here, to talk to me."

Cynthia's mouth curved in a sly smile. "Don't be ridiculous. He didn't do any such thing. That was just a rumor. And guess who started it?" She beamed proudly. "All I had to do was *say* he'd called from California, and it was all over the hospital in no time. And you believed it, like everyone else."

Duffy's stomach heaved. The room was so white . . . so white . . . and so cold . . . nothing but cold whiteness everywhere. And Cynthia, her face a pale, icy mask, seemed to belong in this room.

"Kit never called?" Duffy whispered.

Cynthia shook her head. "Of course not. How could he?"

Duffy recoiled against the wall of metal. She didn't want to know why Kit couldn't have called. Didn't want to know . . . didn't want to hear . . .

"You switched the elevator signs? You sent my wheelchair down that hill and attacked me in the shower? It was you the whole time?"

"Took you long enough to figure it out," Cynthia said. "Maybe that fever has lowered your IQ, Duffy. What did you *think* all those weird sounds in your room that night meant? I tried to be quiet, but Kit was . . . uncooperative."

Her voice was completely cold, matter-of-fact, unfeeling. Cynthia . . . so kind, so helpful, so dedicated . . . Cynthia . . . not Dylan, not Smith, not Amy . . . it had been Cynthia who had tried to kill her.

But *why*?

Kit . . . something to do with Kit, who was in California now.

How could it have anything to do with Kit?

Duffy's eyes searched frantically for a way out of the white room. But the only means of escape was the door through which she had entered.

And Cynthia was barring the way.

"Duffy," Cynthia said softly, leaning closer to her prisoner as she withdrew her hand from her pocket, "don't you want me to refresh your memory about Kit?"

Duffy's eyes, wide with alarm, were on Cynthia's emerging hand. Teeth clenched tightly to keep them from biting her tongue in half, she shook her head vigorously . . . no. No!

"Shame on you, Duffy. Kit was one of your best friends. I would think you'd be more concerned about him than that."

The hand wasn't empty, as Duffy had known it wouldn't be. Her terrified eyes remained fastened on it as it slipped from the edge of the pocket.

Cynthia's fingers were wrapped around a long, nasty-looking hypodermic needle.

Holding the wicked-looking needle high in the air, Cynthia smiled and said, "Well, I'm going to tell you about Kit, anyway." She glanced around the room. "I think it's very appropriate that I tell you in this room." Her cold smile widened.

"Because this is where I brought him after I killed him."

Chapter 24

"I killed him, Duffy," Cynthia repeated when Duffy made no sound. "And I brought him here."

Duffy had made no sound because sound wasn't possible. Her voice had abandoned her, left her body the second that Cynthia's flat, emotionless statement registered.

Killed him? *Killed* Kit?

No. No, that wasn't true. It couldn't be.

But Duffy saw the look on Cynthia's face — cruel and sharp and mean.

Kit . . . Kit wasn't in California, registering for film school? He wasn't thinking about calling her, writing her a long letter telling her all about his coast-to-coast trip?

Kit was . . .

Kit was . . . *dead*?

Duffy's mouth opened wide and her piercing, anguished scream split the air.

"No," she cried, facing Cynthia, tears pooling in her eyes. "No, you couldn't have. You wouldn't. Why would you? *Why?*"

Cynthia had flinched at Duffy's scream and taken an involuntary step backward. Now, she pressed closer again. "Because he knew," she said calmly.

Duffy couldn't stop crying. Kit . . . Kit dead? "Knew what? What did he know?"

"He knew it was my fault Latham died."

Duffy shook her head, trying to clear it. "Latham? Victor Latham?" The newspaper article. "You killed *him*, too?"

Cynthia's voice lowered to a nasal whine. "I didn't *kill* him, Duffy. It was an accident. But that wouldn't have made any difference to the hospital board." Her thin lips twisted angrily. "They'd have seen to it that I never saw the inside of a medical school. Never mind that I've studied my head off, that I'm a good worker. All they would have focused on was that their precious benefactor was dead and it was all my fault. My whole life would have been ruined. Forever!"

"What did you do to Victor Latham, Cynthia?" Duffy forced the words out. Dizzy and sick, she couldn't bear to hear another word. But she had to know.

"Nothing. I swear, nothing!" The whine droned on: "I was just reading his chart one day. I know we're absolutely forbidden to touch them, but I knew how important Latham was to the hospital. I thought his chart might give me a clue about getting close to him, getting on his good side. I knew if I did that, he'd put in a good word for me at any medical school in the country." The voice became sullen. "And it would have worked, too, because a note on his chart said he wasn't allowed to smoke. I'd heard him complaining about how he missed his cigars, so I figured I'd buy some and sneak them into his room. That would have made me his friend for life."

The pale blue eyes filled with rage. "But just then Kit came along. He was delivering a pair of nurse's shoes to that twit with the ponytail. He made some comment about me being too nosey for my own good, and I tossed the chart back into place. But not before Kit saw the name on it."

" 'Latham?' " he said. " 'Isn't that the big shot who has that mansion out on River Road?' "

Cynthia stamped one foot, momentarily snapping Duffy out of her shocked daze. "He noticed the warning sticker, too."

"Warning sticker?"

"Latham was allergic to penicillin. The hospital uses a little round red sticker on a patient's chart for dangerous allergies. Kit saw it. I knew he'd put two and two together when Latham's death made the news."

She's right, Duffy thought in a daze, Kit would have. And he would have gone to Cynthia and asked her questions.

"What did you do to Mr. Latham?" she repeated in a whisper.

"I put his chart back in the wrong place. It was Kit's fault," Cynthia said sullenly. "He got me all rattled, sneaking up on me like that, and I just dropped the chart into the chart table."

"You put the chart back in the wrong spot?"

Duffy shook her head, uncomprehending. "But you told me yourself the nurses always check the names on the charts, so how could that hurt Latham?"

Cynthia's upper lip curled in a sneer. "They're *supposed* to," she said, her voice hard and unforgiving. "But sometimes when things get really busy, they don't. I accidentally put Latham's chart into Mrs. Creole's slot. She was on penicillin. For an infection. The order's right there on her chart. The night Latham died, we had a couple of nurses out with the flu so two nurses came up from the city. They weren't familiar with the patients. One of them gave Mrs. Creole's penicillin to Latham. It killed him. He was so much better that he wasn't on any monitoring equipment. By the time someone checked on him, he was already dead."

"And . . . and Kit said it was your fault," Duffy breathed.

"But it wasn't!" Cynthia cried. "The nurse who had Mrs. Creole's chart must have dropped it into the only empty slot when she brought it back, without checking the room number. That empty slot was Latham's. So later, she gave *him* Mrs. Creole's penicillin, and left the room. She never saw what the penicillin did to him. She got blamed for what happened."

Duffy, knowing it well, said, "Kit wanted you to tell someone about the chart mix-up, didn't he?"

"He said I had to go to Dr. Crowder, the head of the hospital, and tell the truth. Get that nurse off the hook, was the way he put it.

"But of course I couldn't do that," Cynthia continued matter-of-factly. Her eyes widened. "I mean, how could I? Telling the truth would have ruined everything. I would have been fired for handling the charts, and I never would have got into medical school, not ever." Her eyelids drooped sadly. "Without medical school, I wouldn't *have* a life. I tried to tell your precious Kit that, but he wouldn't listen. And the hospital's being sued by Mr. Latham's survivors. So I'd be blamed for that, too. Everyone here would hate me."

Duffy, watching in awe as Cynthia's expression changed from anger to injured innocence thought, *Oh, God, she's insane. She's as crazy as everyone in the hospital thinks I am.*

"Cynthia," Duffy whispered, "where is Kit?" Eyes wide with fear, she glanced around the room. "Is he here? Somewhere?"

"No. I couldn't leave him *here*, Duffy. Why, my goodness, somebody would have *found* him! I had to get him out of here." There was great pride in Cynthia's voice as she announced to a white-faced Duffy, "I put your friend and his car in the old quarry."

Chapter 25

"The quarry?" Duffy's voice was barely audible. Imagining her friend lying deep in the quarry's cold, muddy water, she shuddered.

"Um-hum." Cynthia's gaze centered on a spot somewhere above Duffy's head and took on a dreamy expression. "It was so easy. He really was leaving town, Duffy. Dylan wasn't lying about that. Kit's car was all loaded up and he was ready to take off for California. Only he stopped off here first, to tell you good-bye and," bitterness seeped into her words, "to warn me that if I didn't promise to go to Dr. Crowder with the truth, he'd go *for* me, as soon as he'd seen you." Her gaze returned to Duffy's face. "He was going to *rat* on me, Duffy," she said in a hurt voice. "I couldn't let that happen, could I?"

"What . . . what did you do?" Duffy, her heart bleeding for the loss of Kit, knew there was no way she was going to be allowed out of this room alive. She had to stall, keep Cynthia talking until she could think . . . think . . . how could she think when her whole mind was still wrestling with the horrible fact that Kit was dead?

"I told him I would go see Dr. Crowder, but first I would take him to your room. And that's what I did." Cynthia smiled. "But I grabbed an empty syringe when I left the nurses' station. I knew exactly what to do with it," she said proudly. "I read a lot of medical books, you know. There's this spot on the back of the neck — "

"I don't want to know!" Duffy screamed. "Don't tell me!" She began crying again. Kit . . . she would never see him or talk to him again. How could that be?

Her left hand involuntarily bumped up against the latch of one of the metal doors. The tables inside the cabinet were designed to slide out. Dylan had said so. Did they slide slowly? Or did they whiz out, like sleds on an icy slope? There was no way of knowing. Could she take a chance? It was so hard to think . . . so hard to plan. . . . But she wanted to *live*. And this wild-eyed, pale-faced maniac in front of her didn't want her to.

"Your friend Kit was in such a hurry to see you," Cynthia continued. "Followed me to your room like a puppy. Right straight to your room. You were dead to the world." Cynthia giggled. "Excuse the expression. You were sound asleep, and he didn't want to wake you. He said he wasn't in any big hurry and he'd just sit on the other bed and wait for you to wake up." Cynthia sniffed in disdain. "He said he couldn't leave town without telling you goodbye. Wasn't that *sweet*?" Contempt laced her words.

The thought of Kit sitting on a bed in her room, patiently waiting for her to wake up, Cynthia about to pierce the back of his neck with a needle full of air, made Duffy sick with anguish. If only she could have stopped it somehow, if she could have pushed the call button.

"But he saw the needle," Cynthia went on harshly. "It was dark in there, but he could still tell what I was about to do. He was sitting on the other bed, and I came up behind him. He saw me lift the needle in the air and he made these noises . . ."

Duffy gagged and closed her eyes.

"I missed the first time." There was regret in Cynthia's voice. "Clumsy me! For a minute there, I thought he was going to get away." Then she brightened visibly. "But he didn't. I tripped him," she said cheerfully, "and he went down on his knees. He sort of whimpered then." Cynthia mimicked Kit's deep voice: " 'Please, no, don't!' But I *got* him!" Her voice was triumphant, almost jubilant.

That joy stirred something in Duffy. Anger began to replace her fear, slowly at first, then more quickly, coursing through her body until it became a rage as red hot as her fever. Cynthia was *glad* she had killed Kit! And she was about to kill again.

Duffy screamed. "No! No, no, no!" echoed around the room, and her arms came up and pushed, with all of her might, shoving a surprised Cynthia backward, where she teetered off balance, her mouth open.

But she didn't fall. And she didn't drop the syringe.

Still, her surprise gave Duffy just enough freedom to dart away, running to the desk to search frantically for a weapon: a letter opener, a pair of scissors, anything . . .

There was nothing. A box of paper clips, a lamp, piles of notebooks and leaflets, and a scattered puzzle of pens and pencils . . . nothing the tiniest bit lethal. But there, in the corner, behind a tall, thick medical book standing on end . . . a can of bug spray. Maybe . . .

Duffy turned to face her captor. Behind her, her hands closed around the can.

"Relax, Duffy," Cynthia said calmly, her balance restored. She began to advance slowly, her eyes cold and determined. "You're going to have a little accident," she said, "and it won't be my fault. All *I'm* going to do is be kind enough to give you a ride home. Isn't that nice of me? Of course, *I* won't be hurt. But you . . ." She shook her head. "You'll end up in a ditch by the road in a fiery car crash. I'll tell everyone you grabbed the wheel out of my hands, that you missed Kit so much you committed suicide. They'll believe me. Everyone thinks you're nuts, Duffy. And I'll say that since I'm not crazy like you, I had the good sense to jump out before the car burst into flames." She raised the needle higher. "And no one will ever be able to tell that you were dead before the car ever went off the road."

Her eyes never leaving Cynthia's face, Duffy moved sideways, back to the wall of steel cabinets. She backed up against them, her hands behind her. This time, she found a latch and opened it. It made no sound.

"Wasn't it nice of Kit to decide to leave town?" Cynthia went on, as if they were two friends having a casual chat. "There was his car, all loaded up. . . . After I killed him, I wheeled him down here in the gurney and then later, when everyone was gone, I wheeled him out to his car and drove out to the quarry." She sighed happily. "They'll never find him *or* his car. The water's too deep." After a minute, she murmured, "Sank like a stone. Took me forty-five minutes to hike back to town. Boy, was I beat!"

Duffy, her hands hidden behind her jeaned hips, held the bug spray can in one hand. With the other, she lifted the latch on a metal door. The door opened easily. It made no sound. She tugged gently. The door moved forward an imperceptible fraction of an inch.

"You're crazy," she told Cynthia, her voice shaking. If she kept talking, she hoped Cynthia would continue to watch her face instead of wondering what her hands were doing behind her back. "You're sick. You need help. Why don't you let me go now?" she begged, fastening her eyes on Cynthia's. "We'll go up and talk to Dr. Crowder. He'll see that you get the help you need."

If she was going to get the door open all the way, she had to move forward several inches. But Cynthia was in the way.

Cynthia's cheeks reddened with rage. "I'm not going to *see* anyone!" she shouted. "I don't need *help*! You're the one who needs help!" And she raised the hypodermic needle high in the air, poised just above Duffy's head.

It was now or never. Duffy's hand holding the bug spray can whipped out from behind her, her index finger on the spray button. Her arm flew up, her finger pressed down.

Cynthia screamed as the foul-smelling mist hit her eyes. Her hands, one still gripping the needle, instinctively flew to her face.

The needle's wickedly sharp point missed her left eye by a fraction of an inch, penetrating with full force the top of the cheekbone. This time Cynthia's scream was one of agony. A thin stream of blood slid down her cheek as the needle protruded from her face like a dagger.

Duffy gagged again, but she knew there was no time to waste in sympathy for Cynthia. Cynthia, her anger fueled by new fury, wouldn't give up now. This moment, with Cynthia temporarily blinded, was the only moment Duffy had.

With her empty hand, she threw open the door of the cabinet and, jumping out of the way, grabbed the edge of the slab inside the cabinet and jerked.

The slab flew out, slamming into a moaning Cynthia, her hands still covering her eyes. It kicked her in the stomach at waist-level, lifting her off her feet with a startled "Uuh!" She flew up and then forward, landing with a scream, facedown, on the slab.

She screamed again and then went limp as she lost consciousness.

The weight of her body hitting the slab sent it whizzing back into the depths of the cabinet.

Her eyes glazed with shock, Duffy reached out automatically and gently closed the door. Then her legs gave and she sank to the cold white floor, covering her eyes with her hands.

Chapter 26

When Duffy awakened in her hospital bed the following morning, four pair of eyes regarded her with concern. Smith and Amy stood on one side of her bed, Dylan and Jane on the other. The sight of the little group jolted her out of sleep.

Then she remembered. She remembered all of it: the pillow over her face, the desperate struggle for air, the body thumping to the floor, the cold, dark journey to the basement, Cynthia's arrival at the morgue and . . . Kit . . . Kit! Kit was . . .

Uttering an agonized moan, Duffy buried her face in her hands.

Her friends moved closer. Amy hurriedly poured Duffy a glass of water, Smith took up a position as close to Duffy as he could get, while Dylan and Jane fixed worried eyes on the patient.

Smith was the first to speak. He looked tired, his dark eyes shadowed by bluish circles. "I'm sorry about your friend," he said.

Duffy lifted her head. "You know? You know about Kit? How did you find out?"

"You told us. It was hard for you to say it, but you did."

Duffy's gray eyes widened in fear. She reached out in sudden panic and clutched at Smith's sweater sleeve. "Cynthia?" she asked.

"It's okay, Duffy," Jane hastened to reassure her. "They took her away. She's gone. You don't have to worry about her."

Duffy exhaled in relief.

"Your doctor was in," Smith told her. "They're going to do some tests this afternoon to make sure the digoxin didn't do any permanent damage. He's pretty sure it didn't. He feels really awful about not believing you, Duffy. The whole staff does."

"It was your fever that fooled everyone," Amy added quietly. "Nobody could be sure that you weren't delirious." She waved her hands helplessly. "We're all really sorry we didn't believe you. And," in a hushed voice laden with shame, "I'm sorry I lost my temper. You must hate me."

"No." Duffy shook her head. "It was all Cynthia's fault." Her eyes filled with fresh tears. "She killed Kit . . ." she stopped, unable to continue.

"They found him early this morning," Smith told her, his voice gentle as he took her hands in his and held them tightly.

Duffy sobbed. A sad, sympathetic silence fell over the group.

She wiped her eyes with a corner of the sheet and asked, "Who found me?"

"We did," Jane and Dylan said in unison. "And Smith. It was his idea to try the morgue."

"Dylan called me," Jane explained. She smiled at him before returning her attention to Duffy. "He asked me about the lab test Dean had done on the pills."

Duffy fixed her eyes on Dylan. So he *had* taken her seriously, after all. But too late. He probably had meant well when he brought the nurse to her in the hall. But she would never feel the same about him again, and she could tell by the look in his eyes that he understood that.

Jane didn't need to know about that part of it. The way she was looking up at him, her eyes so full of admiration, she'd never blame Dylan, anyway.

"I *told* Dylan," Jane went on, "that it had all been a gag, but he wouldn't drop it. So finally I told him what Dean had found out and Dylan screamed, 'Duffy was right!' and hung up. That's when I knew it hadn't been a joke, after all. And I knew you were in trouble, Duffy." Her violet eyes reflected hurt. "Why didn't you tell me the truth? I could have helped."

"Then you would have been a target, too." Duffy forced a weak smile.

Jane's eyes glistened with unshed tears. "Oh, Duffy," she said, "I'm so glad you're okay."

And Smith smiled and said, "I wouldn't mind having you in *my* corner, Quinn."

Duffy turned to Jane. "You came to the hospital last night?"

Jane nodded. "I really was feeling crummy . . . bad headache. But when Dylan hung up like that, I knew something was wrong. So I threw on some clothes and raced over here. When I got to the fourth floor, I found Dylan and Smith and Amy hunting all over for you."

"We could tell you'd been in a battle with someone," Dylan said. "Your room was a mess. So we started searching. It was Smith's idea to try the basement."

"We found you on the floor, crying for your friend," Smith told Duffy. "You were really out of it, and at first, you couldn't tell us what happened."

"But you finally did," Amy said. "It was all very disjointed and it took us a while, but we finally figured out that Cynthia was behind one of the doors." Her face was very white. With gratitude in her voice, she added, "It was Smith who found her, and he wouldn't let Jane and me see."

"She tried to kill me," Duffy said. "Like she . . . like she killed Kit." Kit . . . she would never see him again, never talk to him, could never visit him in California.

"When I told you what Cynthia had done," she asked slowly, thoughtfully, "why did you believe me? You could have thought I was the one who did the attacking, that I finally flipped out totally and went after her with the hypodermic needle. Why didn't you?"

"Because we know you'd never do that," Jane said quickly. "And anyway, I knew about the digoxin. And we all knew Cynthia had access to your medication."

"We called the police," Dylan added, "and they sent divers out to the quarry." He hesitated, and his voice was low and reluctant as he added, "They found Kit right away. He was still in his car."

Duffy gasped in pain. She began crying again, quietly, unaware of the tears sliding down her cheeks.

"I can't believe he's dead," she whispered. "What am I going to do without him?"

There was a sad, awkward silence, and then Dylan and Jane said, in one voice, "We'll be here, Duffy." And Amy added in her soft, sweet voice, "Me, too."

And Smith gripped Duffy's hands more tightly in his own and fixed his dark eyes on hers and said solemnly, "I can't take your friend's place. I didn't even know him. I wish I had. But maybe, after a while, I can make a place of my own."

Duffy was too tired to answer. But maybe, after a while, he could . . .

Smith stood up. "This girl needs rest," he said sternly. "I want this room emptied *pronto*."

Nodding obediently, Dylan and Jane and Amy turned to leave. Smith leaned down close to Duffy and said, "It's okay now. You can sleep. You can start putting all of this nasty business behind you and close your eyes. It's over. It's really over."

Feeling safe, surrounded by people who cared about her and wanted her to get well, Duffy closed her eyes.

And slept peacefully.

About the Author

Diane Hoh is the author of *The Invitation*, *The Accident*, *Funhouse*, and *Slow Dance*. She grew up in Warren, Pennsylvania, "a lovely small town on the Allegheny River." Since then, she has lived in New York State, Colorado, and North Carolina. She and her family finally settled in Austin, Texas, where they plan to stay. "Reading and writing take up most of my life," says Ms. Hoh, "along with family, music, and gardening."